THE OTHER LIFE OF MARY ABRAMS

James Edwards III

THE OTHER LIFE
OF MARY ABRAMS

James Edwards III

Kravitz & Sons
INNOVATORS IN PUBLISHING, MARKETING AND ADVERTISING

Kravitz and Sons LLC
1301 Farmville Blvd, Suite 104
Greenville, NC 27834

Published by Kravitz and Sons LLC.

ISBN: 979-8-89639-338-2 (sc)
ISBN: 979-8-89639-337-5 (e)

Library of Congress Control Number: 2025915173

Chapter 1:

State College Building

The November fall day was overcast with a cool breeze that directed paper cups and trash into the courtyard of the state college building. There, you could see a male shadowy figure staring through the second floor window.

His concentration was broken by the chatter of energetic students parading down the hallway coming his way.

I hope this doesn't become a downpour, he was thinking, *maybe just a little drizzle.*

"Hey professor! Did we get the okay for *D.C.?*"

"Not yet! We're still waiting, Mr. Daniels. After the professor's answer, he led them into the classroom. Would everyone please take their seat!

The young college kids scrambled to their chairs.

"Quietly please! " said Professor Hans.

Turning and walking over to the podium, the professor asked, "why is it that your generation insists on removing the proper titles from the English language, Mr. Daniels?"

"Excuse me, Professor? " said Larry.

"Yes, that's what I'm trying to do; it's *Washington DC*! Mr. Daniels, *Washington DC*! "

"Oh! ...ok that's cool!" said Larry Daniels, massaging his right hand.

The Other Life of Mary Abrams | 1

"Class! The field trip to *Washington DC* is still scheduled. We will wait patiently for our confirmation day; please turn to page 21 in your textbooks."

Dressed in a brown polyester suit with a white shirt, no tie and black loafers, Professor Hans was a exchange teacher in his mid-60s from Israel with *a Doctorate in Political Science and Theology*. His definitive view of the world was influenced by his studies in Greek and Roman history. This caused him to believe that the world with all its governmental laws was for the good of mankind. A short man of stature with curly black hair and mysterious gray eyes, olive-colored skin that hung on a round plump frame that fit his personality.

"Would someone read the first two paragraphs of chapter 12?" Professor Hans asked.

A softspoken young woman began reading with the rhythm of a poet.

"The foundation of the government under one man was a requirement to continue the advancement of the Roman empire. It was Gustavus who would be the one person great and powerful enough to control the Senate, the mob and the legions. Gaius Julius Caesar Octavianus Augustus rose above all the great Romans before him and he alone outlasted his political oppo-nents; he reformed a corrupt government and stabilized a system in disarray.

The fall of the Republic was inevitable, but fortunately for Rome the right man came along at the right time and he rose to be the first Roman Emperor."

This voice belong to Maggie M. Werks, a science major with wavy red hair, hazel cat eyes and a model figure that spoke with evidence she worked out. Although she was adopted, her parents were very liberal and wealthy.

As she read the last sentence her voice faded into the silence of the room.

"Thank you! Miss Werks," said Professor Hans, turning the pages of his notes.

Looking up, he stared at the clock hanging over the chalkboard, making a ticking noise with each sweep of the secondhand. It challenged the hissing sound of the old radiator in the corner. The outside wind whistled through the cracks in the glass and fought to get into *the classroom.* The 2 | James Edwards III

fluorescent lights in the ceiling showed yellow faded paint on the walls.

But the light was not bright enough to show the abandoned corners of the room, fallen paint chips lying on the old wooden floor that creaked when one walked across it. Suddenly, a window shade rolled up from the outside forces against the glass.

"Mr. Daniels, would you please pull that shade down'" asked Prof. Hans, startled by the noise.

The young man slid out of his chair and walk over to the window, reached up and pulled the shade back down. Turning around slowly he caught the eye of Maggie Werks. Winking at her, he expected a flirtatious responds. But she just looked puzzled and turned away.

Larry Daniels, coming from a broken home, was raised by his mother who struggled to make ends meet working at local bars. Daniels, a handsome 23-year-old future pro athlete, stood six-foot-one with blue eyes, blonde hair and a muscular build with large hands that enabled him to catch a football. His physical prowess delivered him the scholarship he needed to attend state college. Having a momentary flashback, he glided to his chair as if he was on a football field.

After the distraction, Professor Hans asked, " do you think that the *Philosophy* of one person is a better choice than a collective effort?"

"Of course not!" said the 19-year-old heavyset young man sitting next to Larry Daniels. "It's always better to have more than one thought process; think about it Professor! Dictators have destroyed this world through their own *philosophies!* "

"Mr. Moss, is it? "asked the professor.

"Yes! Dr. Hans," said Bill Moss.

"Well! Mr. Moss, don't you think that individuals have to encourage the minds of the masses?"

"Yes they do sir, but there is still the need for everyone to sit down together and see what's best for the whole."

The Other Life of Mary Abrams | 3

"I think you might be right Mr. Moss, if not right close to it," said the professor, slowly turning away from Moss's convictional stare.

Now Bill Moss was a close friend of Larry Daniels since high school but the two of them were really opposites. Larry being athletic and Bill overweight, coming from a family who owned a chain of hamburger places, he had no interest in physical activities. Moss spent most of his time eating at fast food places and playing video games; occasionally he would help Larry with his homework, standing 5-foot-10 and tipping the scales at 250 pounds, with brown eyes brown hair, styled in a '70s Rod Stewart look that matched his clothing. His asset was the exceptional intellect he had when it came to computers.

Some of the students didn't agree with Moss and began moaning, yelling and talking out of turn, while a low distorted female voice was trying to be heard. Interrupting the melee, she yelled out.

"Professor Hans! If the original idea came from one person, then wouldn't the people be carrying out the philosophy of this one individual,"

said Mary Abrams.

"Can I answer that Professor?" said Maggie Werks, waving her hand in desparaion, determined to be heard.

The professor saw the showdown coming, but decided to let the two students make their points.

"You can attempt to answer that, Ms. Werks " said the professor, smiling.

"Well! The way I see it professor, although the original ideal might be from one person, when several people sit down and began to dissect the thoughts of the individual and reassemble his original idea, it becomes a collective issue with the influence of many different minds."

"Very interesting, Ms. Werks," said Professor Hans, nodding in response.

Maggie had a class before with Mary Abrams but the two 20-year-olds didn't see eye-to-eye. It wasn't that they didn't like each other; they just rubbed each other the wrong way. Besides, Mary could hold her own with Maggie as far as stature. Mary Abrams, growing up on a farm in the Midwest, moved to New York when she was 11 after her parents sold the farm to 4 | James Edwards III

get in the real estate business. With no siblings she stood 5-foot-7 with a shape of a New York model. She was a habitual jogger and captain of the ladies swim team. Her auburn hair was set on a perfect symmetrical face with lips that curled up inviting to be kissed; her deep brown eyes gave a hypnotic stare that invited you into her thoughts.

"But …it's still one original thought Professor," said Mary, interrupting Maggie

"Yes it is, Miss Abrams. Yes it is!" said the professor, walking back to his desk.

Mary, who was sitting up front to the left of Maggie, turned around and smiled with a *gotcha* look. Staring back and eye squinting with vindictive thoughts, Maggie sighed and turned away.

"I think we will stop here in Chapter 12." said Professor Hans, taking a deep breath. Class, let me remind you to make a list of all the things that you will need for the *Summit in Washington DC*; again let me stress how important this meeting is on the world stage. The United Nations is host-ing leaders from all around the globe to come to *Washington DC* to resolve some of the world's crisis: wasted energy, food shortages, healthcare, global pollution etc. etc."

"Excuse me Professor," said Glenn Taste, chewing gum.

"Yes! Glenn," said Dr. Hans, looking over his bifocals.

"My observation is mankind only needs food, shelter and clothing to exist."

"You would think that, " said Professor Hans, looking at the 19-year-old, "but I'm afraid the world is a little more complex!"

"Does it have to be, professor?" said Glenn Taste, tapping his pencil on the desk.

"Is this another extended classroom debate Mr. Taste?" said Professor Hans, walking over to Glenn to intimidate him.

The students broke up the conversation between the two with boos and yelling.

The Other Life of Mary Abrams | 5

"Shut up Glenn!" yelled Larry Daniels.

"Perhaps tomorrow, Mr. Taste," said Professor Hans. "Class dismissed!"

At that command, the students clambered to their feet and began laughing and talking as they bumped and shoved each other leaving the room. Glenn Taste came from abusive alcoholic parents who couldn't keep a job, which made him somewhat of a loner. He lacked some social skills because of the drunken brawls his parents had. He was a skinny kid with a personality that reflected a lot of bullying by other students in elementary school. Standing 6'3 and 165 pounds, with green eyes and long brown hair that he kept in a ponytail, he had an obsession with numerology and astrology, sometimes feeling that fate worked against him. He just wanted to fit in.

As the last student faded out of sight. The Professor thought to himself, *it's going to be a challenge taking this group to Washington DC.*

The subway from the state college building was just a few blocks away and the Professor always enjoyed the walk to the train. Locking up the classroom, briefcase in hand, he made his way down the stairs to the exit.

Reaching the subway, Dr. Hans stood in the coolness of the underground.

He could feel the vibration in his feet as the steel Trojan horse ran the opposite of his destination; the air smelled of electricity as the train finally came his way, slowing down to a halt. He boarded the train and notice an old homeless looking woman at the back, so he decided to sit at the opposite end near an elderly gentleman. *Not many passengers tonight*, he thought, *just enough quietness for a nap.* The Professor loved dozing on the ride home; he considered it therapeutic. As he drifted into a light sleep, the stress of the day began to leave as the train rolled out of the station. The sound of the wheels on the tracks created a low roaring noise that induced sleep fif-teen minutes later.

"Gentlemen," Hollered the 75-year-old homeless-looking woman as she began walking toward them from the rear of the train.

Taking a seat across from Dr. Hans, she sat next to the stranger.

6 | James Edwards III

"My friends for five dollars, just...! Five dollar I will tell you your future."

Wakened from his nap, the Professor and the stranger looked at one another and smiled, knowing that this was a routine hustle on the A train.

"I can tell you the good things or the bad things whichever you prefer!"

said the 75-year-old woman to the stranger sitting next to her. Shaking his head, the non-verbal response told the vagabond stranger that he wasn't interested. Looking at Dr. Hans, she said, "What about you?" Wanting to appease the elderly woman, hoping she would go away, the Professor reached in his pocket and said "I don't need to know my future but here's a donation."

"Well... I wouldn't say that... " said the old lady. "Everyone needs to know where they're headed."

"Okay ma'am-" said the Professor but before he could finish his sentence the psychic started in.

" Yes....!" said the 75-year-old-woman. "I see your future … Your future involves travel? Also you will meet people that you have known before.

There's something in your past that compels you …"

At that point she stopped; pausing for several seconds she said "have you ever been bitten by a snake?"

Surprised at her question, Professor Hans responded quickly. " No …

Never!"

"If you haven't," said the old lady, "be careful … and one day you will understand the dreams."

Looking bewildered, Proessor Hans stood up and made his way to the exit door.

"125th Street," said the computerized voice.

Looking through the window. The Professor could see 125th St. coming into view. "Ma'am, …sir " said Dr. Hans,."Have a good evening."

Pondering what the old lady said, Professor Hans thought to himself, *dreams, bitten by a snake that's crazy*, exiting the train, He walked the last block to the familiar brownstone apartments.

The Other Life of Mary Abrams | 7

Walking up the steps, key in hand, he opened the door to the hallway; another flight of stairs placed him in front of apartment 12.

"Here we are," said the Professor, opening the door and closing it behind him, glad to be home. He felt secure standing there in the dark.

Noticing a flashing red light coming from his home telephone, he immediately went to it.

"It must be a voicemail, " he thought to himself. Turning on the light he walked over to the sofa and plopped down near the phone, pushing the red button, he heard a voice say, "Dr. Luas Hans, we have scheduled you and your students to leave New York Wednesday the 23rd on Flight 125

at 9 p.m. Please be at the airport at least two hours early. If you have any questions please call me, *Ambassador John Dorn* at 206-457-5322."

"Yes!!!" said Professor Hans, "Let me call the students right away!"

8 | James Edwards III

Chapter 2:

The Departure

The night was clear from the early morning rain, allowing the stars to display a beautiful light show against a dark blue sky, accented with the moon shining like a soft spotlight leading the taxicab to LaGuardia Airport.

"So, do you fly often?" said the cab driver cheerfully.

"Not much!" Professor Hans replied.

"Where are you headed?" said the inquisitive cabbie.

"Washington DC!"

"And what's in Washington DC besides those knuckleheads on Capitol Hill?"

"Oh my friend!" said Dr. Hans, "You haven't been keeping up with the news. Haven't you heard about the 11 man, 11 days Summit?"

"Well! I'm afraid I haven't," said the driver.

"Really!" said the Professor. "We must believe that mankind can change, as long as we are willing to do so and analyze our problems." Pausing, he said, "If we fail, then we are doomed! Solving mankind's detrimental problems is what the forum is about, 11 men, 11 days, hoping to stop the world's catastrophic destiny."

"Good luck with that!" said the cabbie, checking the meter.

The Other Life of Mary Abrams | 9

"Yes …" said Prof. Hans, "We're going to need it. Would you excuse me for a moment while I make a personal call?"

"Sure!" said the cab driver, looking in the rearview mirror.

Prof. Hans took out his cell phone and begins dialing.

"Hello! … Hello?" said Dr. Hans in a low voice, almost a whisper.

"You have reached Dr. David Hunter. Our offices are now closed.

Please leave your name and number and we will return your call as soon as possible," the answering machine announced.

"Dr. Hunter! This is Dr. Luas Hans. Sorry to call you after hours but I'm having those dreams again. I'll be out of town for a few days but you can reach me on my cell phone. Please call me! Thank you."

As the Professor was hanging up, the checkered yellow cab rolled up to the entrance doors of the airport.

"Ok! Here we are sir," said the driver, turning the interior light on.

"Thank you," said the Professor as he paid the cab driver and exited the cab to the sounds of thunder from the jet planes arriving and departing.

Entering the terminal, Professor Hans made his way through the airport, finding himself in front of the overhead departure screen. The screen read, *Flight 125-Gate 11 departing 9:00 p.m.*

"Aw yes, there it is," said the Professor. Checking his ticket, he started the long walk down the terminal. Smelling the aroma of pizza, the Professor reflected back to when he was a child in Israel. His mother always made homemade pizza on Saturdays which became a tradition.

Should I stop and get a piece? thought The Professor. *God knows I don't need it.*

As the Professor continued the debate with himself, it wasn't long before he reached Gate 11.

Sitting his bags down, he heard a familiar voice.

"Hey Professor, you made it! " said Glenn Taste.

"Yes, I did Mr. Taste." Said Professor Hans looking perplexed. "Where's the rest of your classmates?"

10 | James Edwards III

Glenn Taste displaying a mischievous smile made the Professor asked again "Where are your classmates?"

Jumping from behind the Professor, Bill Moss yelled, "Professor Hans!

Glad to see you could make it!"

Caught by surprise the Professor responded. "Wouldn't have missed it for the world, Mr. Moss!"

Bill Moss laughed while he hid the Scooby-Doo mask he was wearing.

"Here they come now!" said Glenn, seeing the rest of his classmates headed their way. From a distance you could hear them chanting, "The gang's all here, Pro-fes-sor!! The gang's all here!"

Professor Hans looked on with a proud smile that a father would have for his children. Getting serious, he called out to each of them in a familiar role call.

"Mr. Daniels!"

"Yo, Professor," responded Larry Daniels.

"Ms. Werks!"

Maggie answered only by smiling and winking.

Turning toward his last unaccounted-for student, Professor Hans stated, "Last but not least, Ms. Abrams!"

Mary smiled and saluted in response.

"May I have your attention please! Flight 125 to Washington DC departing from gate 11 in 30 minutes."

Professor Hans looked at his watch. "All right everyone, 30 minutes!"

The smell of food began permeating the nostrils of Bill Moss. "Hey Larry you wanta go for pizza?"

"Naw! Not hungry, " said Daniels, setting a 15-minute alarm on his cell phone.

"You all heard that!" said Moss. "So when he's dying of starvation at 30,000 feet, I'm not sharing!

"You and pizza!" said Maggie. "There won't be nothing left!"

"Maybe bird crust, " said Larry, digging in his pocket.

The Other Life of Mary Abrams | 11

Looking up at Maggie, Larry began laughing uncontrollably, which became contagious.

Mary Abrams looked at the two and shook her head. "All right guys give him a break!" she said, protecting Moss. "And speaking of breaks, where's the restroom? That's where I'm headed," announced Mary.

"It's downstairs!" said Bill Moss pointing.

"Thanks Bill!" said Mary, heading toward the descending escalator.

"Hey Mary, wait up!" said Moss, running to catch up with her.

Hesitating for a moment, Maggie and Larry Daniels decided to follow Bill and Mary down to the first floor.

Picking up a magazine as he sat down, Professor Hans ignored Glenn Taste staring at him.

"I guess it's just you and me," said Taste, putting a rubber band around his ponytail.

"That works for me," said the Professor, opening the magazine.

Glenn took a moment of silence and said. "You know Dr. Hans, I study astrology and I see something major about to take place. It's written in the stars."

Looking over the magazine, Professor Hans focused in on Glenn, saying, "A mind is a terrible thing to waste, young man." The stern face slowly dissolved into a smile, contrary to the expression on Glenn's face, his mouth hanging open.

The crowded airport was a maze of people standing in lines like domi-noes. Some facial expressions showed anxiety of a routine that caused them to be robotic. Although, there was one exception to the rule: the 40-ish tall, thin African American man standing at the balcony overlooking the first floor dressed in a black business suit, with matching tie and hat. He noticed Mary and Bill when they got off the escalator. Watching from the second-floor, he stood statue still, starring intensely at the college students. Reaching into his pocket he looked around and then pulled out a small pair of binoculars.

"I'll see you upstairs in 10 minutes Mary," said Bill Moss, headed toward the pizza counter.

12 | James Edwards III

"Ten minutes Bill!" yelled Mary and "no pepperoni," as she moved through the maze of people only to find a child's doll lying on the floor. A few feet away she saw a child pulling away from her mother looking for something. Mary picked up the doll and called to the child's mother.

"Excuse me Miss!" said Mary "Your child dropped her doll!"

"Oh thank you so very much," said the stranger. "She's crazy about this doll!"

Meanwhile Bill Moss was standing in line at the pizza counter. Feeling the anxiety of flying growing in his stomach, Moss began cramping and decided he better go relieve himself.

Looking for the rest rooms, he saw a unisex sign; rushing toward the sign, he noticed Mary talking to the lady with the little girl.

Oh I should have known, Bill thought to himself. *She would be talking to somebody, just a people magnet.* Hurrying past Mary, he entered the washroom 20 feet away; rushing into the stall, he forgot to lock the door.

The child's mother thanked Mary again and said goodbye. Mary checked the clock on the wall and then saw the unisex sign ahead. As she opened the door she was greeted with Bill 's gastric discharge coming from the stall.

" My God! Excuse me," Mary said. Leaving quickly she went in search of another restroom.

The African American stranger on the balcony was still watching Mary.

His eyes were fixated on her with repute. Seeing her go into the rest room, he started down the escalator stairs. Distracted by all the passengers he didn't see her come out. The mysterious man pushed and shoved his way through the crowd toward the washroom. Arriving at the door he started knocking, not hearing anyone, He pushed the door open.

"Mary … Mary Abrams?"

Bill Moss in the middle of relieving himself responded to the echoing voice.

"Mary? There ain't no Mary in here, asshole " said Bill Moss.

The Other Life of Mary Abrams | 13

"Oh! I'm sorry sir," said the African American, darting out of the restroom.

Who the hell was that? thought Moss. Tearing toilet tissue off the roll.

He cleaned himself and pulled up his trousers, leaving the stall and walking over to the face bowl. Bill washed his hands and fanned them dry. Taking a moment to comb his hair. He thought to himself *don't have much time.*

Rushing out of the bathroom, he heard on the intercom, *"Paging Bill Moss!*

Please return to Gate 11 immediately!

"Are they serious?" said Moss. "I still got seven minutes." Bill hastily walked through the congestion of people back to the pizza parlor. Approaching the counter, he saw there was no one in line.

"Thank God! No one's here, " he said to himself. " Could I have two slices to go?" Bill asked with urgency.

"Sure you can!" said the waitress. She gathered the pizza, put it into a brown bag and handed it to Moss.

Bill paid the lady and told her, "keep the change I'm in a hurry." Turning toward the escalators he dodged an elderly couple in the way and ran up the steps. Seeing the last passenger at the departure door, he hollered to the flight attendant, "Here I am!"

"Well! We've been waiting on you, Mr. Bill Moss I presume?" said the woman in uniform. "Yes!" said Moss sheepishly. The flight attendant escorted Bill down the carpeted ramp to the huge *747.*

14 | James Edwards III

Chapter 3:

The Flight

The whistling sound of the turbine engines endorsing the power of the Jet Plane caused vibrations in the floor rams. This made Moss more apprehensive about flying. Taking his final steps with the flight attendant, he made sure no one could see the pizza he was hiding under his jacket. Entering the *747*,Bill was greeted with the sounds of cheers and applause.

His classmate Larry Daniels, hollering over every one said, "Hey Mossy where'd you go? *Italy?*" Moss's embarrassment was revealed in his face as it turned a blushing red. Happy to see the Professor waving to him, Bill rushed down the aisle. Catching the eye of Larry Daniels, he gave him a middle finger gesture.

"Back here Bro...!" said Glenn Taste waving to Bill.

Walking back to Glenn, he saw an empty aisle seat.

"Take a seat Bro!" said Glenn.

"If he can fit in it," Injected Maggie sitting next to Larry Daniels.

"I heard that, Maggie! " said Moss thinking of an incident when he was a teenager, when he wanted to ride the roller coaster but wasn't able to fit in the seat. With his classmates laughing at him, he struggled, but managed to get seated behind Maggie Werks.

The Other Life of Mary Abrams | 15

The Professor reassured the flight attendant that everyone was accounted for. Turning to his students, Professor Hans waved in the air to get their attention and told them to settle down.

Sitting in front of Larry and Maggie were Professor Hans and Mary Abrams. Turning around and getting on her knees in her seat. Mary mocked the Professor."That's right class!" said Mary, laughing. "Settle down."

This generation! thought Professor Hans. "Okay Ms. Abrams! Please turn around and buckle up."

"May I have your attention please! " said the head flight attendant.

"We have special guests flying with us to *Washington DC.* On board with us, Ambassadors James and John Dorn, guest speakers at the 11 Man 11

Day Summit. The passengers clapped with enthusiasm, welcoming the ambassadors on board.

"How about that class?" said Prof. Hans, excited to have the sponsors of their trip on board.

"Well we should have a good flight!" Glenn Taste said three rows back.

"What would make you think that?" said Bill Moss trying to fasten his seatbelt.

"Because bro!"said Taste, with a chuckle, "they don't wanta lose their precious cargo."

Finally getting his seatbelt fastened, Moss turned to Glenn and asked,

"And what might that be?"

"Really Moss! Do you have to ask?"

"Oh yeah, I get it! Safe flight equals, Ambassadors on Plane. I guess I'm nervous. You know I don't like flying and on top of all that, you guys made fun of me for being late."

"Come on Mossy it wasn't that bad," said Glenn, fidgeting with his ponytail.

"Don't call me that!" said Bill. "If you want to be helpful, give me some paper and something to write with. I gotta tell Mary something *.* " Digging through his backpack on the floor, Glenn handed Moss paper and pen.

"So that's why you became the Airport Pizza Delivery Man," said Taste grinning.

Taking the paper and pen Moss began writing, pausing for a few seconds to give Glenn a middle finger gesture.

The note said: " Mary, I need to talk to you, as soon as we get airborne.

Don't worry I got the pizza." Folding up the paper he tapped Maggie on the shoulder.

"Give this to Mary." Taking the note with some curiosity , Maggie handed it to Mary sitting in front of her.

Mary took the paper and unfolded it. "Mary I need to talk to you as soon as we get airborne." Reading the note to herself, her words trailed off. *What the hell!* Mary thought. *This man is obsessed with food.*

She glanced over her shoulder as she crumbled the note. Noticing, Professor Hans asked, "Problems?"

"Not at all," said Mary, brushing her hair out of her face "Everything's cool!"

"Attention please. I'm Head Flight Attendant Liz Brown. Please turn off all electrical devices and buckle your seat belts." The other flight attendants demonstrated how to use the oxygen masks while Liz talked. We will be pushing away from the terminal in five minutes."

The doors closed on the big *747* readying the plane for flight. Mo-ments later the plane pushed away from the loading terminal and started making its way to the tarmac. The *747* shuttered and shook while the turbine engines whined and cried for more air. "This is air traffic control to flight 125! Please move to runway 0010." The large plane slowly moved into position, making a right turn onto the tarmac and coming to a stop while waiting for final instructions.

"This is air traffic control! Good evening Flight 125. You have clear skies with a south-westerly wind at 30 knots. Nothing but stars in the sky.

You are clear for takeoff! Have a good flight!" The Captain revved the engines to their takeoff speed and released the clutch . The jumbo jet lurched The Other Life of Mary Abrams | 17

forward and accelerated down the runway, leaving a trail of vapor and noise, climbing to 30,000 feet.

"This is your captain speaking! We have now reached our cruising al-titude of 3 3 0, speed, 500 knots with a cloudless sky. Estimated time of arrival to Washington DC is approximately an hour and 20 minutes. Again, welcome aboard Flight 125." With the end of the Captain's announce-ments, the seatbelt sign went off. Passengers began to relax, moving about the cabin as the parade of food carts began to roll down the aisle.

Larry Daniels stood up stretching his 6-foot-1 frame. "Hey Mag!" said Daniels, "I'm going to the lavatory; get me a Coke."

"Where's the money Mr. Football?" said Maggie looking up at Larry with a smile.

"I'll pay you when I get back," said Larry Daniels, as he stepped over Maggie and hustled down the aisle.

Leaning forward, Maggie whispered in Mary's ear, "why don't you come back here and sit? We can chat while Larry is gone."

Although Mary knew Maggie had something up her sleeve, she decided to play along. Standing up, she moved to the chair behind her.

With curiosity in her voice, Maggie asked, "So tell me Mary, you and Bill got a thing going on?"

"Hell no!" said Mary. "Don't be an asshole Maggie! It was just a fucking note."

Professor Hans, overhearing their conversation, told the girls to "hold it down back there." At that moment, Larry Daniels returned, to the smile of the Professor.

"I guess it's my turn?" said Professor Hans. Fighting against the momentum of the plane, Dr. Hans manage to stand up and shuffle down the aisle way.

Standing there patiently, Larry asked Mary with a Don Juan smile,

"Uh … can I get my seat back? Or you want me to sit in your lap?"

"You wish buddy!" said Mary, standing up and getting out of his way.

She moved back to her assigned seat.

18 | James Edwards III

Bill Moss watching, saw the opportunity. Standing up, he scurried to the empty seat next to Mary.

"Hey Mary did you read the note?" Moss said, wondering what she thought of it.

"Yes I did Bill. Why so secretive? It's only pizza!"

"Fuck no! I wasn't talking about pizza! When we were in the airport.

I was using the toilet and some guy stuck his head in the door and called your name."

"What? Bill Moss! Have you lost your *freaking mind?* Who the hell would be looking for me in a restroom especially a man? And watch your mouth."

"*Calm down!* I'm just telling you what I heard." Moss said feeling he was fighting a losing battle.

"And what did he want?" asked Mary looking totally baffled.

"How am I supposed to know?"

"Okay, what exactly did he say?" asked Mary with a serious expression.

"He said, 'Mary? Mary Abrams?'"

"And what else Bill?" asked Mary, as her memory rolled backwards, thinking about her cousin Elizabeth, who loved to play guessing games when they were 12 years old.

"That's it!" Moss exclaimed.

"That's all!" said Mary in a high pitched voice.

"Yeah that's all, but don't you find it strange: a man looking for you in the airport bathroom?"

"Yes I do," said Mary, "but I find you even stranger, so you can get up out of Professor Hans' seat, Mossy!

"Hey don't call me that!" said Bill "What about the pizza? It's here in my jacket." Moss pulled out the limp pizza in a grease-soaked bag. Mary looked at it with displeasure, thinking to herself, *mmm ... that pizza has been through a marathon, running around under Bill's jacket.*

"Help yourself Bill!" Said Mary. "I'll get something off the food cart."

The Other Life of Mary Abrams | 19

Bill got up and went back to his seat two rows back. A couple rows ahead of Mary, there was a big commotion in the aisle way. The flight attendant Liz was asking about a passenger who has passed out.

"What happened?" said Liz, the flight attendant.

"I don't know? " said the passenger sitting next to the elderly woman.

She just stopped talking and slumped in her chair. The flight attendant checked for a pulse and didn't find one.

She immediately started down the aisle to the flight deck. Coming her way was Professor Hans with Ambassador John Dorn in tow. Liz acknowledged the Ambassador and the Professor and continued to the flight deck.

Larry, seeing them coming, pulled out his cell phone and began videotaping. Finishing, he slid down in his seat and said, "Check it out Mag!

Professor Hans must have met one of our sponsors."

"So I see," said Maggie. Fixing her hair, she stated. "What a handsome guy."

Rejecting her comment, Larry sat silent.

Ignoring all the commotion, Glenn Taste sitting in the back with Bill Moss became excited as he looked out the window. He saw a little ball of light in the night sky.

"Hey bro!" said Glenn, reaching over shaking Bill Moss.

Startled by Glenn's excitement, Moss asked "What's up with you?"

"There's a little ball of light out there that has been following us for the last 15 minutes."

"What!" said Moss. "You mean like a UFO?"

"That's exactly what I mean!" said Taste looking out the window again.

Moss sat up in his seat but was afraid to look.

"You're full of shit, Glenn." Moss said, refusing to look.

"What the hell you guys talking about back there?" said Maggie, closing the magazine she was thumbing through.

Bill leaned forward and whispered to Maggie, "he's gone crazy, those astrological charts and numerology stuff have screwed up his mind. Now he's seeing things."

20 | James Edwards III

"I'm telling you it's following us, if you don't believe me just look out the window . "My God!" said Glenn. "It's growing and coming straight at us."

"That's enough!" said Moss becoming frightened. Standing up and moving into the aisle, Moss stood next to Maggie as she was leaning out of her chair trying to see what was the commotion down the aisle. The Professor and Ambassador John Dorn were about to pass the stricken woman when the jumbo jet, having a malfunction, dropped 100 feet causing the lights to go out. Sounds of panic fill the dark cabin of The Plane with outbursts of religious cries of "oh my God!," "Jesus!," "Lord help us!"

and low audible prayers.

"This is your captain speaking! Please! Everyone return to your seats.

We are experiencing an electrical problem." Rushing down the aisle way to the Ambassador, a tall dark figure asked Are you okay?"

"I'm fine!" said the Ambassador, standing in the dark with Professor Hans.

" I'm very sorry," said Ambassador John Dorn to Professor Hans. Turning to the students in the dark, he said, "I would love to meet all of you in the light," laughing nervously, but I will meet all of you in Washington DC at the conference," a male voice behind the ambassador announced.

"Sir! You have to return to your seat now!" he said with authority, taking the ambassador's arm . Ambassador John Dorn left with his assistant, passing the Head Flight Attendant with the captain headed down the aisle to the unconscious passenger. Listening intensely to the voices in the dark.

Bill Moss was shocked when he recognized the voice that came to rescue the ambassador.

That's the voice I heard in the bathroom, he thought to himself while trying to see which man was speaking. But the dark plane prevented it as he heard more voices coming his way.

"I'm telling you Captain this woman has expired! *She has no pulse!* " said Liz the Head Flight Attendant. As they arrived at the sick woman's seat, flashlights in hand. The Captain felt the lady's neck for a pulse and mumbling to himself, then he said "I feel a heartbeat."

The Other Life of Mary Abrams | 21

"That's impossible!" said the flight attendant, feeling the woman's chest herself.

A voice coming out of the darkness said, "I feel fine. What's all this foolishness about?"

Shining the flashlight in the face of the elderly woman with the silver-grey hair, the Captain was surprised to see a big euphoric smile on her face.

"How do you feel?" said the Captain, moving closer.

"I'm fine!" said the woman, "I must've passed out."

"Can you tell us your name?" said the Captain, checking her pulse again.

"Yes..! It's Marga-ret Walker."

"Very good! " said the Captain. Turning to the flight attendant he asked in a low voice, "Is she a wheelchair passenger?"

The flight attendant whispered back, "Yes she is. She can't walk at all."

Turning back to the senior citizen the Captain asked, " Ma'am would you like some water?"

"Water would be fine young man. Oh and by the way, you have soft hands." she said, smiling at the Captain.

Smiling back at her, the Captain turned to Liz and said,"thank God for small miracles. And I'm sure you can handle it from here." Leaving, the Captain rushed down the aisle to the flight deck. With all the commotion you could barely hear Glenn Taste screaming .

"It's coming! It's gonna hit us! It's gonna hit us!" The ball of light hit the *747* and went through it, causing the Jumbo Jet to shake violently. Suddenly the lights came back on and the plane smoothed out. Cheers and applause from the frightened passengers passed through out the plane like a wave at a baseball game.

"This is your Captain speaking! We apologize for any inconvenience we might have caused you. As you can see we have resolved the problem, no pun intended. We will be arriving in Washington DC in 10 minutes.

Please stay in your seats and fasten your seatbelts."

22 | James Edwards III

Feeling reassured the passengers calmed down. Wiping the perspira-tion off of his forehead the Captain asked, "What the hell happened?"

"Just one of those nights, Captain" said the co-pilot, setting the gauges.

"Yeah well it's time to put this big bird on the ground," said the Captain lowering the flaps.

"This is Flight 125 to air traffic control asking for heading."

"This is Air Traffic Control! We got you Flight 125, set heading 004 .

Welcome to Washington DC."

The large jumbo jet descended through the atmosphere, breaking the clouds and revealing the city lights. Two miles ahead the airport was to the right. The Pilot banked the large wings of the *747* and continued descending until the wheels touched the tarmac.

The Other Life of Mary Abrams | 23

The Arrival

The *747* touched down with the cheers of the passengers. Slowing down, it found its way to the arrival gate. Reaching the safety area, the plane was hooked up to a truck and towed in to the terminal. The expansion bridge came out like a slow moving caterpillar and connected to the plane. The Doors opened and the passengers began to disembark . Professor Hans stood up to address the students.

"Well class! We all made it safe and sound. Make sure you don't leave anything."

All the students began gathering their belongings, except for Glenn Taste.

"Hey Glenn!" said Bill Moss, taking his backpack from the overhead storage. "You better start getting your stuff!"

Hearing Moss to the left of him, Glenn turned and said "I can't see!"

"What do you mean you can't see?" Bill said, looking confused.

"I can't see God dammit," said Glenn Taste feeling around "I'm blind!"

Calling up front to the Professor, Bill Moss yelled "Dr. Hans, I think we got a serious problem!"

Walking back to them, the Professor asked, "What is it?"

"The ball of light! I can't see; I'm blind!" said Glenn Taste, with panic in his voice.

"What?" asked the Professor. Baffled by Glenn's blindness Dr. Hans blurted out, "Everything's gonna be all right. We're going get you to a hospital."

The Professor told the students to exit the airplane, while he took the arm of Glenn Taste and led him down the aisle, stopping at the exit door to inform *the pilot* of Glenn's situation. Leaving the plane they continued through the terminal to the baggage area. The Professor instructed the students to gather the rest of their belongings off the carousel.

"Class!" announced Dr. Hans. "Glenn and I will catch a cab to the hospital and you guys excuse me, guys and gals, will go pick up the rental van and meet us there. Understood? Okay! Now … Who has an available cell phone?"

The four students took out their cell phones and start posing with them.

"You know class … Any other time that would be funny but not now, please! Not now!" said Dr. Hans with intimidation. The students refocusing took the matter more serious. Larry Daniels took a card out of his wallet and handed to the Professor. "I'll call and tell you what hospital we're at!" said Professor Hans.

Mary, Maggie, Larry and Bill answered in sympathetic harmony,

"Okay!"

Saying goodbye, they told Glenn to hang in there and that he would be okay. The young college students followed the car rental sign to the escalators and then to the second floor. Seeing the rental counter they walked over and stood in line. Coming from the next counter over a male voice caught their attention.

"Excuse me," said the tall African American man in his 40s. "I'm Samuel Moore an aid for Ambassadors John and James Dorn. I'm here to pick up keys for a Black Cadillac SUV Sedan."

"That's him! That's him!" said Bill Moss, becoming nervous. "That's the voice in the dark on the plane, the same voice that called Mary's name in the airport bathroom."

26 | James Edwards III

"What?" said Larry, listening intensely. "Maybe? Well! Yeah. I guess he does sound like one of them on the plane."

Mary Abrams, looking perplexed and moving behind Maggie asked,

"Are you sure? What could he possibly want with me?"

"Well I'm not sure … Why don't we ask him?" said Maggie, wanting a confrontation.

"Not funny," said Moss taking pizza out of his jacket and throwing it in the trash. "This guy could be a terrorist or something."

"How could he be a terrorist?" Said Maggie Werks, her voice becoming brazen. "He's the *Ambassadors' Aid;* you heard him."

"Next In line!" said the young brunette working the counter. Bill Moss, unfolding the rental papers and stepped to the desk.

"Hi there," said Moss "We have reservations for a passenger van under the name of *New York State College located in New York."*

She took the paperwork from Moss, rumbled through some drawers and handed him the keys while giving him directions to the rental cars.

The African American Man had begun to exit the rental car office, headed for the parking lot. Daniels hurriedly ushered the group into a circle.

"Hey look guys! I got an idea! Let's follow him and find out where he's staying."

"Why?" said Mary Abrams "You wanta go to jail!"

Getting excited, Maggie blurted out, "I think it's a good idea. Why not?"

"Well I don't think it's a *good idea,* " said Mary, shaking and biting her nails. "These are high officials and we're stalking them."

"Maybe Mary's right! This isn't such a good idea," said Bill, as perspiration began to show on his forehead."

"Let's take the vote … Who's in favor of stalking?" Daniels said with a nervous laugh. Maggie raised her hand.

"Mary?" said Larry, "the vote's on you."

Standing there silently, staring with apprehension, she said nothing.

The Other Life of Mary Abrams | 27

"How about you Bill?" said Daniels. "Majority rule."

Feeling awkward and pressured by Larry, Moss slowly raised his hand half way. Glenn, looking on, responded, "What the fuck."

"Cool!" said Larry. "Let's go before he gets away."

The students rushed to the exit doors out into the parking lot looking for the rental van.

"Where is Row D over here!" said Maggie. The rest of the students ran over to her with the keys and opened the door. As they were about to get in they saw the Ambassadors' Aid driving by.

"Hurry up! Get in! " said Daniels jumping into the driver's seat. The students scrambled into the van while Larry started the rental. Buckling his seat belt, he pulled out of the lot. Driving down the ramp, they saw the black SUV pass by in front of them.

"There he is!" said Maggie. "He made a right turn."

Getting to the exit, Larry made a right as he saw the black Cadillac SUV turning left at the next corner.

"Turn left at the stop sign!" said Maggie, not taking her eyes off the black SUV.

"This is insane!" said Mary Abrams, gripping the door support.

"Hey Mary, we're doing this for you!" exclaimed Bill Moss.

Feeling her blood pressure rising, Mary kicked the back of Moss's seat and blurted out, "You're not doing this for me asshole!'"

"I mean, well I didn't mean."

Laughing out loud Maggie asked, "What did you mean? Mossy!"

Interrupting them Daniels said, "Hey guys cut it out! Let's just stay focused."

The students' passenger van weaved in and out of traffic hitting some potholes but finally catching up with the black SUV .

"Not too close, not too close!" said Moss, sitting up front with Larry.

The black Cadillac SUV accelerated down the asphalt pavement coming into a tree-lined street with mansions on both sides. The homes were 28 | James Edwards III

perfectly aligned like checkers on a checkerboard, with iron rod fences and bright security lights that could light up a football stadium. These security measures protected the representatives, whose countries accumulated the wealth to build these monstrosities. Looking like modern-day pyramids, they displayed and boasted the architectural genius of man. The van approach the white mansion on the right with Roman columns. The black iron gate screech as it opened up to the black Cadillac SUV. The truck continued down the long road until it disappeared behind the mansion. The students had been following the black SUV from distance. Minutes later, the college students arrived, slowly rolling up in front of the mansion.

"Where are we?" said Mary Abrams, with a quiver in her voice.

"If I could take a guess," said Moss, "I believe we're on *Embassy Row.*"

Maggie, admiring the beautiful homes, asked, "Is this a special street?"

"It's the street where all the Ambassadors live when they come to this country," said Larry Daniels as he stared out the window, noticing a *No Parking, No Standing* sign.

Bill Moss, looking surprised, turned to Larry and asked, "How did you know that?"

"Mossy! My man, I do pick up a book sometimes," said Daniels, winking at him.

"How many times I gotta tell you guys not to call me that!" said Moss pounding the dashboard.

Smiling, Daniels said, "Sorry … Kiddo!"

"Hey guys!" said Mary. "Someone is peeking out the window."

"Let's go Larry! Before someone comes out," Moss said, shaking his leg nervously.

"You're all a bunch of chickens," said Daniels, as he checked for on-coming traffic.

The dark blue passenger van slowly pulled away from the curb, made a U-turn, and headed back to the National Airport DC. The city streets had a few late-night tourists running around. But for the most part, the The Other Life of Mary Abrams | 29

city had unplugged . Flashing neon street signs periodically lit the inside of the van, revealing the perplexity on the faces of the college students.

"Fuck!" said Larry Daniels. "This trip is starting out crazy."

"What time is it?" Said Maggie Werks, putting on lip gloss.

"Almost midnight," said Mary Abrams, yawning as she checked her cell phone.

"We haven't heard from Dr. Hans," said Moss, sounding worried.

"I hope Glenn is all right," said Mary, leaning back against the head rest.

"Yeah me too," said Maggie. "I second what Larry said …or would that be *I third*."

Laughing, she said, "Crazy.

"Yeah! Really crazy!" said Bill Moss, "You know when we lost power on the plane, I thought we were gonna crash."

"Thank God the power came back on," said Mary, "or they would have been reading about us back home."

"Yeah thank God!" said Larry. "So what the hell do you think caused Glenn to go blind?"

"Don't know," said Maggie." He said he saw a ball of light."

"Do you really think he saw something?" asked Mary, turning to Maggie.

"Who knows what he saw?" said Larry. "You were sitting next to him, Bill. What did you see?"

"To be honest, I thought he was bull shitting," said Moss. "So I never looked."

As the van retraced its route back to National Airport, Larry Daniels' cell phone rang. Taking out his phone, he heard the Professor.

"Hello!"

"Hey Professor, it's Larry! "

"Yes Larry, we're at MedSTAR Washington Hospital Center. The address Is 110 Irving Street if you have any problems use the GPS system."

"Okay Professor, we should be there in the next 15 to 20 minutes."

30 | James Edwards III

"Hey!" said Mary sitting up "Ask him how is Glenn."

"Professor Hans? Is Glenn okay?"

"He's doing somewhat better. I'll let him tell you himself when you get here," said the Professor clearing his throat.

"Okay Prof," said Larry hanging up and taking his bluetooth out of his ear.

"He's somewhat better," Maggie said with an inquisitive tone in her voice. "What the hell does that mean Larry?"

"Hey look Mag! … I'm just telling you what the Professor told me. In the next 15 or so minutes you can ask him yourself." The young college students began to feel the wear and tear of the trip. The 8-passenger rental van became the student's refuge from the unusual events of the day, making its way through the downtown century-old streets toward the MedSTAR

Washington Hospital Center.

The students reclined their seats back, putting up their feet, trying to catch a quick nap but the night flight had taken its toll and they found it hard to drift off. Breaking the silence Mary asked "Bill are you sure the Ambassadors Aid is the same voice?"

"I swear! That's the same guy that stuck his head in the bathroom."

"So you saw his face?" Mary asked excitedly.

"No! But I know that's the same voice."

"Okay Bill!" said Maggie. " Can we just leave it alone for tonight?"

"Hey guys, what's the address?" said Larry, breaking the conversation up.

"110 Irving Street," said Moss. " Just a few more blocks. Make a right at the stop sign at the top of the hill and then a left."

"You must be familiar with DC," said Larry, adjusting the heat.

"Yeah, I used to come to restaurant conventions with my dad. It seemed like it was always in DC," said Bill, pondering the thought.

The dark blue rental made its way through the fall night, past the caramel-colored treasury building, to the hospital The landscaped trees out in front, with golden-colored leaves still hanging on, clambered for The Other Life of Mary Abrams | 31

attention. Pulling up slowly in front of the emergency center, they saw Professor Hans through the glass door.

"Somebody go get 'em," said Larry Daniels, turning the ignition off.

"Mary … You sleep?" said Moss, shaking Mary. With no response from Mary, Moss tried waking up Maggie.

"Maggie!" hollered Bill. Sound asleep Maggie didn't respond either.

"Hey Bill, cut the bull shit! Just go and get 'em," said Daniels, tired of waiting.

"Yeah, it's always me," said Bill Moss, pushing the unlock button and opening the passenger door. He climbed out and headed for the emergency entrance. A refreshing gentle breeze blowing into the van induced Larry into a light sleep. Awoken abruptly by the opening of the side door, Larry saw Professor Hans and Bill Moss helping Glenn into the van. The co-eds woke up glad to see their classmate and showed compassion to Glenn Taste with hugs and pats on the back. After securing Glenn in the van, the Professor and Moss climbed in behind him.

"So Glenn, what did the doctor say?" asked Mary, being inquisitive.

Displaying a drug-induced smile from the hospital medication. Glenn started rambling incoherently.

"Excuse me," said Professor Hans, "the doctors don't think it's perma-nent and I think that's great news. Now! It's been a long day and were all tired and need some rest. We 'll have plenty time to talk tomorrow over breakfast. Mr. Taste will share my room tonight. Let's go, Mr. Daniels,"

said the Professor. Larry buckled his seat belt and started the van. Turning on the GPS system, he followed it to The Hey- Adams Hotel. Forty minutes later, they arrived.

"All right gang !" said the Professor." I'm gonna go in and get the hotel cards. You guys start unloading. Bring everything into the lobby and I'll give you your room key. The students gathered their belongings. Struggling with all the suitcases and bags, staggering from fatigue, they finally make it to the lobby. Professor Hans handed Maggie and Mary key cards 32 | James Edwards III

301 and the guys 304, while he would stay in 310. Squeezing in the elevator with all the luggage, they reached the third floor, finding their rooms. They retired for the night.

The Other Life of Mary Abrams | 33

Chapter 5:

The Schedule

The gray fall morning was ushered in by a bright yellow sun peeking its head above the horizon. Coming off the Potomac River was a warm calm wind, that helped create the Washington DC temperature of 70°. Long gone were the apple blossoms that bloomed in the spring, yet the trees refuse to give up their red, yellow, and orange leaves that displayed a kalei-doscope of colors showing off the beauty of the city.

" You're listening to 98.1 WASH-FM," blared the radio.

"What! The hell," said Larry Daniels, sitting up in bed "Hey Moss!

Moss! Turn that damn thing off."

Bill Moss, in a mouth-drooling deep sleep, continued snoring. Daniels took a pillow off the bed and through it, hitting Moss in the face.

"Hey what the fuck!" said Moss, half-asleep knocking things on the floor trying to find the *radio off* button.

"What time is it?" Moss said, wiping the drool from his mouth.

"Time for all good men to come to the aid of their country," said Larry jokingly as he got up and went to the refrigerator. "Hey man the fridge is full of beer and food. Who stocked it?"

"Compliments of the hotel because we're guests of Ambassador Dorn. I don't think they know how old we are," said Moss, looking back The Other Life of Mary Abrams | 35

at the clock radio. "Hell, it's only 8 o'clock," Moss said, falling back across the bed.

Wearing only his underwear, Daniels closed the fridge, walked over to the middle of the room and began doing push-ups.

"Yeah!" Said Daniels. "The right time for a early morning run. I think I'll call Maggie and Mary and see if they want to go for a jog."

Ignoring Larry, Bill Moss began to drift back off to sleep and began snoring.

"Hey Moss … Moss, Did you see my cell phone? Man … You're worthless! Oh here it is." Finding his cell phone under his clothing bag, Larry dialed Maggie.

"Hello! Maggie? Hey, this is Larry. You and Mary wanta go jogging?"

"Mary isn't here Larry. She went to early morning Mass at St. John's Church but I'll run with you."

"Cool!" said Daniels, happy to be alone with Maggie. "Meet me in the lobby," he said hanging up.

Hanging up, Larry rushed into the bathroom for a quick shower.

Coming out, he took a pair of jogging pants and a shirt with the school's logo on it out of his suitcase. He hurriedly put them on along with his running shoes. Grabbing his key card, he headed out of the door. Catching the elevator to the first floor, he saw Maggie standing in the lobby looking radiant; her wavy red hair was combed back and braided in a ponytail and she was dressed in Kate Hudson jogging attire with Nike Zoom Terra kieger running shoes. She looked like an ad for sports magazine cover.

"Hey Mag! Looking good!" said Larry, drooling.

"Thanks Larry," said Maggie, blushing and pinning her hair back.

"So where are we running to?" asked Larry, putting on his sunglasses.

"I checked the local maps and we're about a mile from the Lincoln Memorial, so I figured there and back is about 2 miles," said Maggie, stretching her arms.

36 | James Edwards III

Still admiring Maggie's figure. Larry was having a man's *waiting to exhale* moment, but he managed to say "I'm up for it," exiting the lobby.

The two took off running.

As they were jogging, Maggie noticed a granite Cathedral-looking gray church. "Oh there's the church that Mary went to: St. John's."

Turning to look and almost tripping, Daniels said, "Cool! It's not far from the hotel."

As they passed the church, early morning Mass was wrapping up.

"In my Father's house are many mansions: if it were not so, I would have told you. I go to prepare a place for you. And if I go and prepare a place for you, I will come again, and receive you unto Myself; that where I am there ye may be also," quoted the Catholic priest. "Let us pray." Mary said a prayer for her classmate Glenn Taste and bowed her head with the other few parish-ioners. The priest gave his blessings and final salutation and church was dismissed.Standing up and walking to the end of the pew, Mary was shocked to see Ambassador John Dorn's Aid coming out of a pew and leaving the church. Her fear would not overrule her curiosity. She rushed down the aisle trying to catch him. When she reached the exit doors he was gone. Walking down the church steps to the sidewalk, she thought to herself, *what's the odds of the Ambassadors Aid and I attending the same morning Mass?* Looking over her shoulder, she started the short walk back to the hotel.

The Hey-Adams Hotel was a caramel-colored building with a French architectural design, nine stories high and housing over 100 vacationers.

Built back in the 1900s it was just down the street from the White House and St. John. Reaching her destination, Mary walked into the hotel lobby to see Professor Hans and Glenn Taste in a jovial hand waving conversation with the concierge.

"Hi everyone!" said Mary. The group of men turned to her with big smiles and sung the words "good.morning."

She could see the excitement on everyone's face even Glenn's. With an inquisitive half-smile, she asked, "why is everyone so giddy?" With no The Other Life of Mary Abrams | 37

response, she turned her attention to Glenn and asked, "Are you all right?"

she said, touching his shoulder.

With a big clown-like smile Glenn Taste said. "It's good to see you."

"Oh my God … You can see!" said Mary, smiling from ear to ear.

"Yes I can!" exclaimed Glenn.

"I'm so happy for you!" Mary said running over to Glenn as she hugged him.

"Thank God!" said Professor Hans, as the concierge agreed by nodding.

"Well tell me! What happened?" asked Mary

Almost too excited to speak Glenn said, "Well! We got up this morning and showered, got dressed and the Professor brought me down to the lobby and had me sit and wait on him while he check the breakfast schedule. Then I heard my name being paged. I called out to the desk clerk and he came over and said I had a phone call. So he helped me back to the desk and gave me the phone. I said 'hello!' And no one said anything for a few seconds, then I heard a voice on the other end say 'Glenn? Glenn Taste?' I said 'yes' and they just hung up. The desk clerk helped me back to my chair. I sat back, closed my eyes for about five minutes and when I opened them again I could see!"

"That's crazy!" said Mary, shaking and jumping with enthusiasm.

"It's a phenomenon., said Professor Hans. "There are many things in life you just can't explain."

"What's going on?" said a sleepy-eyed Bill Moss walking up from behind them.

Mary yelled out, "Glenn got his sight back."

"What!" said Moss, looking dumbfounded.

"I can see, bro!" said Glenn Taste excitedly, as he did a little dance.

"His sight came back!" Said Professor Hans. "Isn't that great!"

"Welcome back Glenn!" said Moss, giving him a fist pump.

"Thanks bro," said Glenn smiling.

"So where are Larry and Maggie?" asked the professor. "Did they come down yet?"

38 | James Edwards III

"I don't know, " said Mary. "I left Maggie upstairs."

As she was speaking, Larry and Maggie were coming through the door.

"Oh! Here they are now," Mary said. Walking up to greet everybody the two joggers showed some signs of fatigue and flushed faces.

"What's going on?" said Maggie wiping sweat from her face. "What time is breakfast?"

"Breakfast is up until 11 o'clock," said Glenn Taste. "So you two need to shower and meet us in the dining area."

Larry Daniels and Maggie, staring at Glenn with their mouths hanging, open realizing his sight had returned.

"Oh … shit! You can see!" said Maggie, fanning herself.

"Watch your mouth!" said Professor Hans, looking stern.

"Sorry!" said Maggie, walking over to Glenn, hugging and kissing him on the cheek.

"Okay … Can't we take this to the dining room?" said Bill Moss. "I'm hungry!"

"Good idea!" said the Professor. "We will all feel better with something in our stomachs."

"Well …. we're gonna go shower, will be back in a minute," said Larry Daniels.

Maggie and Larry caught the elevator upstairs, while the rest of the group headed down the hallway to the dining room. Thirty minutes later, Larry and Maggie had joined their classmates.

The Other Life of Mary Abrams | 39

Chapter 6:

The Discussion

The decor in the dining area was of a French influence: gold and white floral wallpaper with diamond bright chandeliers that showed a beautiful blue plush carpet that you sunk into. The floor-to-ceiling French windows allowed the outside light to display the craftsmanship on the reddish oak provincial chairs placed at the dining tables. Embers popping and crackling in the fireplace forced the heat to move across the room with the elevator music, creating an atmosphere of serenity

With everyone seated, the professor stated: "I'm glad everyone could make it for breakfast. Does anyone have any concerns that need addressing?" The group could hardly wait to tell the Professor about the Ambassador's Aid.

"The Ambassador's Aid!" blurted out Mary Abrams. "He was in church with me this morning"

"What?" said the class in unison, giving Mary their full attention.

"What Ambassador's Aid?" asked Professor Hans leaning, forward as he listened intensely.

"Ambassador John Dorn's Aid!" cried Bill Moss. "This is the same guy!

I heard in the restroom at LaGuardia."

"Wait a minute! Hold on," said Professor Hans with a stern voice.

"What guy in the airport restroom?"

The Other Life of Mary Abrams | 41

"It's sort of a long story," said Mary Abrams. "You see, Bill told me that some man stuck his head in the unisex restroom and ask for me."

"He asked for you for what? "said the Professor straightening his glasses and wiping his mouth with a napkin.

"I don't know," said Mary looking puzzled, "but this same guy came to early morning Mass."

"You're losing me," said the Professor, fidgeting in his seat.

Larry, Maggie and Glenn all tried to talk at one time.

"Hold it! One at a time," said Professor Hans as the dining room waitress came over and interrupted the conversation. She took their food orders and disappeared into the kitchen.

"Okay," said the Professor. " Where were we?"

"Look! Professor Hans," said Maggie. "It's a black guy following us around asking for Mary.

"Wow! I missed a lot." said Glenn Taste, looking dumbfounded.

"So! Who can explain all of this?" sighed the Professor.

"I think I can," said Daniels. "Moss was in the bathroom in New York and a gu *y* came in and asked for Mary. Then Moss heard the same voice on the plane when the power went out. Also at the rental car, Moss recognize the *guy's* voice and it was Ambassador John Dorn's Aid. We overheard him say his name was *Samuel Moore.*"

"Who happens to be *African American*," said Bill Moss, taking a sip of orange juice.

Addressing Mary, the Professor said, "I think I got it! And now this *guy* showed up for Mass this morning and you were there."

"Well class let's be realistic. No one has said anything to you. Have they?"

Bill Moss, hollered out. "Yeah! But he asked for Mary in the bathroom."

"But you didn't see him?" said Professor Hans. "Did you?"

"No … I guess I didn't," Moss said feeling defeated, sitting back and slumping in his chair.

42 | James Edwards III

"Anyone else?" said Professor Hans.

Maggie raised her hand. "I think we should look out for this *guy* and if he comes back around we should go to the police."

"I'm with Maggie!" Said Larry Daniels, pounding the table.

Glenn Taste started waving his hands, getting the attention of his classmates.

"This all sounds creepy to me," said Taste. "See, I told you guys something was going on with the planets."

"Please Glenn!" said Mary. "Don't say *see...*"

Maggie, Larry, and Glenn turned their heads back and forth like confused puppy dogs and then started laughing.

Bill, not finding the conversation funny, said "Yeah okay, you guys go ahead and laugh but I'm the one that heard him ask for Mary. At least we know where he's staying," His voice trailing off.

"What!" said Professor Hans, turning to Bill Moss.

Larry realized Moss was not thinking about the brevity of what they had done. Urgently he chided in: "I think he said, 'Are gays allowed to stay here?'" He winked at Moss, while the rest of the students tried to keep a straight face.

Professor Hans, looking stunned and bothered, asked. " Why wouldn't they? Under the law everyone has a right to stay where they want! It's written in the Constitution, ladies and gentlemen," the Professor said seeing the waitress coming with their breakfasts.

"On that note," said the Professor, "I think we should end this conversation for now. I'm sure you all are ready to eat, and here comes the food."

"It's about time!" said Bill Moss, as the waitress handed out plates of stacked pancakes dripping with butter, Golden Brown Tennessee linked sausages and yellow scrambled eggs. Mozart's "Eine kleine Nachtmusik"

2nd Movement flowed through the speakers filling the dining room, stimulating hungry palates. As Dr. Hans finished up his last cup of coffee, he could feel his cell phone vibrating.

The Other Life of Mary Abrams | 43

"Excuse me class, I have to take this phone call. Let me know what you guys and gals plan to do after breakfast. I'll have the desk clerk put your daily schedules under your door every morning." Standing up and feeling well fed, the Professor exited the dining area, heading back to his hotel room.

"Yes! Sorry to keep you waiting," said Dr. Hans.

"Dr. Hans? … David Hunter. I got your message. So! Tell me what's going on?"

" I'm having nightmares again! Not only am I dreaming I'm blind, I'm having real life experiences with blind people. One of my student became blind on the flight here."

"I'm sorry to hear about your student, but it's only a coincidence. Remember there only dreams. When are you returning?"

"Eleven days," said Dr. Hans, feeling somewhat reassured.

"Okay! Call me when you get back and we'll set up a appointment. Remember they're only dreams," said Dr. Hunter.

"Thank you, Dr. Hunter. I'll see you when I get back." Hanging up and opening his hotel door, the Professor went inside. Taking off his jacket and loosening his tie, he laid his cell phone on the table and it began to vibrate. Picking the phone up he said "Hello Dr. Hunter?"

"No! It's me," said Glenn Taste. "We were calling you, to tell you we were gonna take the old town trolley tour around Washington DC."

"Ok." said Professor Hans, taking off his shoes. "How long is the sight-seeing tour?"

"A couple of hours," said Glenn Taste.

"That's fine," said Dr. Hans. "Make sure you remind everybody the summit starts tomorrow morning at 9 a.m. So … Don't stay out too late and be careful."

Glad to get off the phone, Glenn Taste said, "Okay!" Hanging up, he relayed the telephone conversation to the rest of the class.

Mary Abrams, combing her hair asked, "Where do we catch the trolley?"

44 | James Edwards III

"Union Station! 50 Massachusetts Street: about four miles," said Bill Moss.

"Really! How'd you know that?" said Larry Daniels, burping.

"I just used my GPS on my cell phone," said Moss, displaying his phone.

"That's cool, bro!" said Glenn Taste, leaning forward and giving Moss a fist pump.

"All right guys!" said Maggie. Can we just saddle up?"

In agreement with Maggie, Mary said "Yeah guys, let's go."

"We're ready," said Daniels and Taste, standing up while Moss ignored them and continued eating.

"Let's go Moss! You've eaten enough," demanded Larry. Moss picked up a biscuit, wrapped it in a napkin and stuck it in his hoodie sweatshirt.

He then followed them as they left the dining room. Going through the lobby to the parking garage they located the Rental. Having a last minute meeting in the parking garage, they loaded the van. Larry and Bill sat up front while Maggie, Glenn and Mary sat in the back. They buckled up while Larry started the van and exited the lot.

The Other Life of Mary Abrams | 45

Chapter 7:

The Trolley Tour

The fall afternoon was a warm stimulating sunny day of 75°, with a powder blue sky that hung strange lenticular clouds over union station. The college students using the GPS system on their phone finally arrived at the tour bus departure center . Pulling up and parking, they began unloading out of the passenger van.

"Holy Mother of Jesus! Look at those clouds," said Glenn Taste, standing in amazement, "I've never seen nothing like that before."

"Me … neither!" said Mary Abrams, looking bewildered, as she shaded her eyes with her hand from the bright sun.

"Wow! Incredible!" mumbled Maggie, staring at the clouds along with Larry Daniels and Bill Moss.

"They look like pancakes," said Glenn. "I told you guys there's something strange going on. My Astrology charts show it."

Larry spoke up. "they're just clouds asshole! Give me a break!" Daniels said, putting on his sunglasses.

Hanging on to Larry's confidence, Bill Moss stated, "That's right! Shit!

They're only clouds." *But*, he thought to himself, *they do look like pancakes*.

"All right guys!" said Maggie. "Now that the pissing contest is over, Let's just get our tickets and get the hell on the bus."

The Other Life of Mary Abrams | 47

"Makes sense to me," Daniels said, walking over to Maggie and putting his arm around her. The couple started walking toward the ticket counter, while the rest of the group followed.

"Welcome to the hop on hop off trolley tour!" said the cashier. "That will be $48 a ticket."

"Damn!" said Taste, taking out his wallet and counting the money he had.

"What's the matter, Bro! Need a loan?" a vindictive, smiling Bill Moss asked.

Checking his wallet again, Glenn found an extra $50. "Naw … I got it Mossy!" He waited for Moss's reaction. Glenn watched as Moss slowly raised his middle finger, giving him his routine finger gesture . The rest of the class ignored the two, bought their tickets and walked over to the black and orange tour bus.

"Welcome aboard! " said the driver, as the students climbed on the bus. Larry Daniels and Maggie Werks went to the back and sat together.

Bill Moss and Mary Abrams sat two rows in front of them across from Glenn Taste. Other passengers began to board the bus, filling up the front seats. The 20-passenger tour bus started up, pulled out of the station, and headed down the road, arriving at Arlington.

"National Cemetery 511 10th Street, northwest … Ford Theater," the driver yelled.

The college students climbed off the bus and started the short trek to the Ford Theater. Maggie and Larry continued their flirtations, lagging behind. The rest of the students entered the theater. The setting was like that of a stage play with original props in place that recorded the assassination.

Realizing the historical value of where they were, they became solemn.

"So, this is how it looked when President Abraham Lincoln was assassinated," said Mary Abrams, with sympathy in her voice.

"Yeah … spooky," said Bill Moss, taking a donut out of his hoodie sweatshirt and taking a bite.

48 | James Edwards III

"Let's go up to the Presidential Box!" said Maggie Werks, with adventure in her voice.

Agreeing, the students climbed the stairs to the second floor.

"Man!" said Bill Moss. "We're actually standing where John Wilkes Booth stood when he shot the President! Where was the Secret Service?"

"Go figure!" said Maggie, thinking about a fight she had in high school. If her chauffeur had been on time, she would have never gotten beaten up. Her mind drifted back to the present. "It was a different time guys."

"Of course it was a different time," proclaimed Larry Daniels, reaching up and touching the Plexiglas that didn't allow tourists to go any further.

"But this was *The President of the United States*. I just wonder why authorities at the time weren't more protective."

"You have to remember, bro!" said Glenn Taste. "John Wilkes Booth was an actor at the theater, so naturally he had the freedom to move about.

This place was converted to a theater only in its latter days. It used to be a warehouse and a church, I think it was built around 1833 maybe? Years later it became *Ford Theater.* And on April 14, 1865, President Lincoln was shot in the head and taken across the street to the Peterson house where he died some hours later."

"Mmm … interesting Glenn!" Mary said, laughing. "We have our own tour guide!" Looking over the balcony through the protective glass to the main floor, she noticed a man standing in the shadows. She turned to her classmates, shaking with fear. "Look! Look down there!" She pointed to the figure of a man near an exit column.

Pulling her hair back out of her face Maggie squinting to see. "I don't see anything."

"Me neither," said Larry and Bill, repeating each other.

Not letting Mary respond, Glenn blurted out. "She thought she saw the Ambassador's Aid."

"Why would you say that?" said Mary, getting nervously upset.

The Other Life of Mary Abrams | 49

Larry, Bill and Maggie stood in silence, but with anticipation waited for Glenn's answer.

"Because … I saw him too!" said Glenn, slinging back his ponytail.

"Are you talking about the *black guy*? *Moore?* " Larry Daniels said, raising his voice.

"Yes!" Mary Abrams cried in frustration as she took tissue out of her purse.

"Okay! Well … we don't see him now?" said Maggie, walking over to Mary, putting her arm around her.

"Are you two sure it was him?" said Bill Moss, his leg shaking out of fear.

"I know what I saw Bill!" said Mary almost in tears.

"Me too, bro," announced Glenn Taste.

Waving his hands in the air to get his classmates' attention Daniels said, "Alright! Everybody just cool out!"

Walking over to Larry nonchalantly, Glenn whispered in his ear, "You need to round them up bro!"

Taking directions from Glenn, Larry suggested that his classmates head back to the tour bus. Leaving Ford Theater , the students went on to their next attraction. Sitting at the back of the bus Larry asked Maggie,

"Do you think Mary and Glenn actually saw somebody?"

"Don't know," said Maggie. "So far this has been a pretty strange trip!"

"Well! I agree with you about … pretty," Larry said, with ulterior motives.

"Yes! The city is pretty impressive," said Maggie. Opening her purse and taking out a diamond studded compact mirror, opened it and began primping and putting on lipstick.

"Not the city Mag! … I'm talking about you!" said Daniels in a serious tone, thinking about all the other girls he could be dating, yet there was something about Maggie that intrigued him.

"Real-ly!" said Maggie smiling and blushing, as she closed the mirror.

"Yeah … You know I always had a thing for you," said Daniels moving closer.

50 | James Edwards III

"Well … Mr. Handsome, I could be persuaded if you didn't have so much baggage, you know, you being Mr. Football and all. Question for you Larry, what about the women that go along with that title? Then there's the NFL draft! You won't have time for me, buddy."

Maggie's expensive perfume began to permeate the nostrils of Larry Daniels. Moving even closer, Daniels put his arm around her. "Mag..! How can you say that?"

"No! Seriously Larry," said Maggie fidgeting, and trying to push him away.

Cupping her chin and turning her face to him. Larry said in a whisper,

"Ba-by! I will always have time for you." Larry's words began to soften Maggie's heart, making it pliable as butter.

"So, you're gonna make time for me huh?" said Maggie looking directly into Larry's blue eyes.

Moving within a half inch of Maggie's lips Daniels said, "Looking into your beautiful hazel eyes, I don't see an hourglass of time, but endless nights of love and passion."

Losing herself in the hypnotic flow of Larry's words, Maggie was gone in silence.

Pulling her to him, Larry hard-pressed his lips upon hers. Feeling the stimulating wetness of each other's mouth, Maggie let out a low audible moan. Pushing Larry back, she began fanning herself with her tour booklet.

"Whew! That's enough of that!" Maggie said, with a flushed face.

Straightening her blouse, she turned around to see if anyone was watching.

"Hey? Mag!" said Larry, touching her on the shoulder to get her attention. "And?" said Larry.

"And what?" Maggie said, putting on fresh lipstick.

"What about the kiss? No physical or emotional stimulation?"

Gazing at Larry, she said, with a slow sexy voice, "Not … bad! Next time use your *tongue.* "

The tour bus driver's announcement on the intercom interrupted the young couple's romantic interlude.

The Other Life of Mary Abrams | 51

"Next stop, Arlington National Cemetery." There was an uncanny quietness as the passengers arrived on the grounds of the Famous National Cemetery, where soldiers, presidents, senators and other famous dignitaries were buried. The passengers began disembarking the tour bus. The rambunctious college students were the last to exit the bus. Catching up with the rest of the tourists, they stopped to listen to the tour guide.

"Starting with the Revolutionary war in 1775, veterans from every American war have been buried in Arlington National Cemetery . Beginning with the Civil War, more than 330,000 of our nation's soldiers and veterans have been interred here. These 624 acres of hollow grounds were dedicated on June 28, 1864 when America was fighting its most costly war.

The first soldier buried here was Private William Christman of company G, 67th Pennsylvania infantry. President Coolidge said long ago, 'The nation which forgets its defenders will itself be forgot.,'" said the tour guide.

"As a country, we will not forget the men and women who sacrificed their lives for our nation and I'm sure you're all aware of the eternal flame that never goes out, which is the gravesite of President John Fitzgerald Kennedy, who was buried here on November 25, 1963, after being assassinated November 22, 1963. I will be taking all of you to President Kennedy's Burial Site. But I must ask you to stay in a tight group, because of the private ceremony underway. We have some dignitaries near the gravesite honoring Boy Scouts with merit badges."

Beckoning the tourists to follow him, he started out toward the grave.

Walking down the pristine sidewalks and beautifully-landscaped lawn, they reached the gravesite where they saw throngs of people watching the ceremony. "Now!" said the master of ceremonies . "We will ask our visiting Ambassador Thaddeus Ivanoff from Russia to present the awards." The Ambassador walked to the podium and began calling names.

"Larry James, Isaac Hester and James Mason. These are some of the outstanding young men that will continue the greatness of America," said Ambassador Thaddeus Ivanoff. "We honor them today with the Eagle 52 | James Edwards III

Scout's badge of merit. Out of the three young boys, Larry James walked with a limp, slowly making his way to the podium with the other two. The three young scouts shook the hand of Ambassador Ivanoff as he congrat-ulated them. Minutes later, the ceremony was over and the college students moved closer to the eternal flame.

"Now! This is very emotional for me," said Maggie Werks. "I did a paper on the Kennedy Assassination, and in my research I found this site was chosen because President Kennedy and his friend Architect John Carl Warnecke had visited the site in March 1963 and the President admired the peaceful atmosphere of the location. After his death in November 1963, the First Lady Jackie Kennedy requested an eternal flame for her husband's grave. It was rumored she drew inspiration from the eternal flame at the tomb of the unknown soldier at the Arc de Triomphe in Paris."

"That's freaking deep!" said Glenn Taste. It reminded him of the time his parents didn't have enough money to bury his uncle Phil. Glenn, putting a rubber band around his ponytail, said "Yeah! They must be spending a hell of a lot of money to keep this flame lit."

"They who?" said Bill. "We're the *they*! This is taxpayers' money at its worst."

Mary Abrams was shaking her head with disappointment, about to speak, when Larry cut her off.

"Just bull shit politics! The gas that has been wasted here could have heated hundreds of homes."

"You … guys! you guys! All of you should be ashamed of yourselves.

Do you know the political impact that this man left on this *nation?* He demanded that the states recognize civil rights for every citizen in this country and he backed it up with the military by sending the National Guard into the South. So show some damn respect," said Mary Abrams, putting her hands on her hips.

Looking at one another, Mary's classmates felt ashamed and embarrassed, some of them turning red-faced, realizing they had made some The Other Life of Mary Abrams | 53

foolish statements. An atmosphere of melancholy fell on the students as they began walking back to the tour bus . Reaching the parking lot, they saw a maze of traffic with lines of people waiting to board different buses.

"Hey guys!" said Bill Moss. "Who's hungry? Let's find something to eat."

Realizing there were hundreds of people preventing their leaving, Moss hollered "Holy shit! Look at all this congestion. We'll never get the hell out of here."

"Anticipation Mossy! Anticipation.! See you gotta think like a football player. Move all the traffic to one side and you'll have a clear path to the goal post," Larry said, flexing his muscles and adjusting his sunglasses.

Maggie, smiling and giving her undivided attention to Larry, pre-tended to have a football. She began mocking him as though they were in a football game. She tried to run past him, but Daniels affectionately grabbed her by the waist.

Mary, looking somewhat surprised, asked Bill, "What's going on with them?"

Hunching his shoulders, Moss said, "Who cares? I'm hungry."

"It's just in your mind! Bro!" said Taste, pulling out a PC tablet and logging something.

"Yeah … The food images are in my mind Glenn, that I know, and I'm trying to get them out of my mind into my stomach," Moss said, looking angry. Mary and Glenn, seeing how upset Moss was, began walking toward the bus, while Larry and Maggie fooled around taking cell phone pictures, later jogging to catch up with the rest of the class. Walking across the street, they saw some tour buses pulling out, looking like black and orange caterpillars making their way down the winding road to different tourist sites. Hundreds of people were left standing in line to board the remaining buses. The college students could hear one of the young Boy Scouts who was awarded a merit badge.

"It's my leg! Grandfather!" Said Boy Scout Larry James excitedly.

54 | James Edwards III

"Ma kO-re," said the elderly short man with gray hair.

The young boy scout started jumping up and down, and then blurted out, "P) N V)N)."

"Hallelujah," cried the grandfather exhilarated, getting the attention of the tourists around them. The old man hugged the young child and they climbed on the tour bus next to the college students' bus.

"Well, glad to see someone having a good time," said Maggie Werks, half smiling.

Looking at Maggie, Larry said jokingly, "They must be Polish?"

"Mmm … They could be Polish," Mary Abrams said, "But they're speaking Hebrew!"

Everyone looked stunned at Mary's response. Glenn commented, "We didn't know you spoke Hebrew!"

"A little bit," Mary said looking out the window, thinking to herself *it's no big deal, you can learn anything online.*

"So, what did he say?" Daniels asked, taking off his sunglasses.

"I didn't … understand all of it, but he said something about his leg!"

"Well! We know the kid had a limp. We saw him walk across the stage," said Maggie.

"The hell with that!" Moss yelled, looking at his classmates. "Can we just get on the bus and get back to the hotel?" Wanting to scold Moss for his rudeness, his classmates decided to let it go, nodding in agreement to board the bus.

"Hey!" said Glenn looking out the bus window, "Look who's boarding next to us!" The young college students scramble to see.

"My God! It's Ambassadors Dorn's Aid!" Mary Abrams said, scrambling to get a better view.

"Where!" said Bill Moss nervously, not being able to see.

"Right there!" said Glenn. "*Mr. Samuel Moore* himself."

"Why the hell is he on a tour bus?" asked Larry Daniels, gripping the back of the seat.

The Other Life of Mary Abrams | 55

"Don't know," Glenn Taste mumbled. "Wait a minute! He's getting back off."

The college students watched as Samuel Moore left the bus next to them and got into *a black Cadillac SUV* double parked. Patrolmen began clearing the traffic for the SUV to leave quickly, moving with an escort through the congested maze of traffic, blowing leaves up in the air as it left.

"Well! Thank God he's gone now!" Mary said, relaxing and sliding down in her seat.

"Would everyone please be seated," said the tour bus driver starting the bus.

The students went back to their original seats feeling the excitement of the day slowly dissipating. After several different tourists stops, the bus reached its destination. End of the line, said the driver. The college students moved in slow motion exiting the bus. They made their way to the van, climbed in and arriving at the Hey-Adams, they exited the rental.

"Hey guys!" said Bill Moss, "I think I'm going to order food up in my room and play some video games. Anyone up for that?"

"I'll take you up on that bro!" said Glenn. "Since I'm going to be staying with you guys."

"Staying with us?" Daniels said with a frown while finger combing his hair.

Maggie chided in with a baby voice, poking fun at Glenn "Awww!

What's the matter? You don't want to stay with the Professor anymore?"

"Hell no!" said Glenn, rubbing his hair back. "He snores!"

"Well," said Daniels, "you better order up a cart to sleep on unless you and Mossy wanta bunk together."

"F-you Larry!" said Moss raising his middle finger and moving away from Larry.

"Alright, alright! Guys," said Mary. "I'm going to check on the professor. Maggie? Larry? Whata you guys gonna to do?"

"We were thinking about grabbing a sandwich in the bar and have a few drinks," said Maggie.

56 | James Edwards III

"That sounds cool!" said Mary with a genuine smile. "I'll meet you guys there after I let the Professor know we're all back."

The group broke up. Bill, Glenn and Mary headed down the hallway to the elevators while Maggie and Larry found the hotel's bar. Catching the elevator up to their floor. Bill and Glenn told Mary they were in for the night. She gave them a hug and then walk to the opposite end of the hallway finding the Professor's room. She knocked on the door. Within minutes Professor Hans opened it.

"Oh … I see you're back?" said Professor Hans, adjusting his glasses.

"Yes, Professor were all back. We're going to hang around the hotel for the rest of the day."

"That's fine," said Professor Hans. "If any of you need anything, just call me."

"Thank you Dr. Hans!" said Mary smiling as she told the Professor to have a good evening.

Walking back to the elevator bays, Mary pushed the button. Within seconds the doors opened and she took the elevator back down to the main floor. Reaching the lobby, she found the bar where Larry and Maggie were.

The atmosphere was quiet with relaxing jazz music coming from overhead speakers and strobe lights that played tag on the walls. Walking into the bar she saw her classmates sitting in a candlelit booth.

"Hey Mary! You made it," said Larry, giggling as Mary approached the booth.

"What's up guys? What are you drinking?" said Mary taking off her jacket and putting her purse on the table.

"Margarita!" Maggie said, laughing as she began feeling the effects of the alcohol.

"Me! Scotch and Coke," said Larry Daniels with some sobriety.

Maggie moved over closer to Larry so that Mary could slide in the booth.

Taking a drink and setting her glass down Maggie asked, "So how's the Professor?"

The Other Life of Mary Abrams | 57

"He's fine! I think he's right at home! Well not at home! But you know what I mean."

"You mean he has the atmosphere of his home," said Daniels, taking a sip of scotch and setting down his glass.

"How so?" said Mary, picking up a menu looking for her favorite chicken wing dings.

"Well, the man lives in a shoebox and act like a recluse. "

"I wouldn't say that!" said Mary. "Professor Hans is just a reserved, intelligent man."

"Reserved for what?" said Maggie, laughing and laying over on Larry's shoulder.

"Don't be judgmental guys. Have some respect for your elders. After all, he has the knowledge we're seeking."

"Yeah … You're right Mary," said Larry, feeling some sentiment. "You want anything to drink?"

"As a matter fact I do! I'll take a half glass of Cabernet," said Mary, looking at the wine chart.

Larry called the waitress over and ordered Mary a glass of wine.

"Changing the subject. What do we do about this Samuel Moore?"

said Maggie, sitting up straight.

"The guy is becoming a pain," said Larry Daniels. "What he needs is a good old-fashioned New York ass kicking. That'll stop him from following us around! Hey … maybe Moss can run his name through the Internet and see what comes up?"

"Great idea Larry!" said Maggie. As the waitress arrived with Mary's wine, sitting it on the table, she picked up the five dollar tip Mary laid on the table and left.

"I … don't know about that!" said Mary, taking a sip of wine. "We don't want to invade anyone's privacy," Mary said with a frown, tasting the bitterness of the wine.

"We're not!" Larry said.

58 | James Edwards III

"We're using information that's available to the public."

"I just don't want to break the law!" Mary said, taking another sip of wine.

The students, feeling more intoxicated and lightheaded, decide to call it a night.

"Well guys! I guess I'll head upstairs," Mary announced, drinking the rest of the wine left in her glass." Standing up to leave she said, "It's been a long day."

"Holdup … Mary! Maggie and I are coming too," said Daniels, struggling to his feet. Maggie slid out of the booth, waiting for Daniels. The two women could see the young athlete had had too much to drink. Each one of them took Larry by the arms to help him walk to the elevators. The three students getting on the elevator headed up to their floor. The mirrored elevator doors opened with Maggie and Mary helping Larry exit.

The three stumbled down the hallway to his room. Knocking on the door, they called out to Bill and Glenn.

"Who is it?" said Bill Moss, with his ear up against the door.

"You know who it is asshole! Open the door!" Maggie Werks yelled.

"Hold on Maggie!" Moss said. Grabbing a pair jogging pants, Moss slipped them on and opened the door.

"Here's your boy! The star athlete of New York State College! " Maggie said, pushing Larry over the threshold into the room.

Moss standing there, looking at Larry drunk, wanted to laugh but instead asked, "What happened to him?"

Mary realized there was some humor in seeing such an agile athlete barely able to stand. "What happened to him is what happens to every human being that consumes too much alcohol," said Mary with a snicker.

Glenn, sitting in the chair playing *Top Spin 4*, paused the game to help Moss walk Larry to the bed. Grabbing hold of the other arm the two young men just let Larry fall on the bed.

The Other Life of Mary Abrams | 59

"He'll be okay in the morning," said Glenn Taste thinking back to the many mornings he found his father drunk on the floor.

"I hope so!" said Mary, noticing the bemused look in Glenn eyes.

"Okay guys we've delivered the package. He's all yours. Mary and I are going back to our room to crash. See you guys in the morning," said Maggie

The young college women exited the guys room and headed down the hall.

"Man. How much you think he had to drink?" Bill Moss asked, staring at Larry passed out.

"I don't know bro. But if I had to guess, I would say quite a bit," Glenn said, standing over Larry and laughing as he slept.

"Yeah. It's been a rough day!" Moss said, walking over to his bed and falling into it. "Aren't you tired of playing video games?"

"Yeah I think I had enough for tonight! Bro, just need some sleep."

Glenn turned off the videogame and walked over to the portable cot.

Seeing the cot brought back memories of him being locked up in a juvenile facility for smoking weed in high school. The facility had cots to sleep on.

"Good night *bro*!" said Bill Moss, mocking Glenn. "See you in the morning."

Coming back to reality Glenn responded, "Yeah bro ... sleep tight.

don't let the bed bugs bite." Back to his memories, Glenn drifted back into his own private world of sleep.

60 | James Edwards III

Chapter 8:

The World Summit

The morning was clear but brought a light frost, causing the Washington American goldfinch to go on strike from its routine of bird singing. The quietness seem to still the landscape as though you were looking at a picture. From the window of he Hey-Adams Hotel, you could see a few soli-tary joggers just beginning their morning run.

"Hey Mary! You awake?" asked Maggie, standing at the window taking in the morning view.

Slowly lifting her head up to see where the voice came from, Mary said

"I am now."

"Well you're missing all the fun!"

"What fun?" Mary asked, yawning and stretching.

"These gorgeous guys! You got to see them!"

"Maggie, Maggie … Maggie!" said Mary, as she turned her back and pulled the covers over her head.

Swooning over the athletic joggers, Maggie began singing *Let Me Be Your Baby Tonight.*

"O … Kay" said Mary, climbing out of bed and shaking her head. Shuffling over to the window, Mary looked out. With a sheepish look on her face, she quietly said, "I see a few potentials. Not bad!"

The Other Life of Mary Abrams | 61

"Yeah, me too" said Maggie, dreamy-eyed as she opened the window.

While the two girls were talking, another group of joggers began running past the hotel with a police escort.Red and blue lights flashed as if they were in a parade.

"Whoa … get a load of this group!" Maggie cried, fixated on the pack.

"I'll take the blonde one."

"The blonde one? How many blonde ones do you need?" asked Mary, yawning.

Looking red-faced and losing her enthusiasm, Maggie said, "Are you referring to Larry Daniels?"

"Yes I am," said Mary, looking very serious. "What's going on with you and him?"

"Mmm, well … Larry's nice but …"

"But what?" said Mary, waiting for specifics.

Maggie, thinking about Larry's moodiness, said, " I know Larry is a football star and has a huge ego but don't you find him to be a little strange at times?"

"No stranger then the rest us. Hell, we're all college kids trying to find our way," Mary said with conviction., focusing her attention back to the runners. She realized these were not your ordinary joggers.

"The guy with the dark brown hair … doesn't he look familiar to you?"

asked Mary.

"Not really and besides who cares!" said Maggie pushing the window open more.

"Honestly Mag ! Don't you see the police lights flashing, They're the Ambassadors. Don't you recognize Ambassador Dorn, the second runner from the front? He was on the plane with us!" Mary cried.

"Holy shit! It is!" Picking up her backpack off the floor, Maggie pulled out a small pair of binoculars. Focusing in on one specific person, she handed the binoculars to Mary.

"Lime green shirt, white jogging pants. Get back!" Maggie screamed as she pushed Mary away from the window.

62 | James Edwards III

"Is that who I think it is? My God!" said Mary, her voice shaking.

"Yeah! Did you see that? He looked right up here at us. Mr. Samuel Moore himself," Maggie said, with some aggravation in her voice.

Maggie reached for her cell phone on the dresser. Turning on the cam-era video she started videotaping. "I think what we need is a nice video of Mr. Moore and when we go to the Summit today we can ask him what the hell is he following us for or I guess I should say you."

"Great idea!" said Mary. "Maybe we can get to the bottom of this bull shit. I have a lot of questions for this Samuel Moore person."

With eyes wide, and thoughts running wild in their minds, the two young ladies were interrupted by Mary's cell phone vibrating, "BZ … BZ

… BZ." Bumping the corner table as she reached for her cellphone Mary answered.

"Mary? Professor Hans. Everyone should be in the lobby at 10:30 The meeting starts at 11:00."

"Okay Dr. Hans! Will be there," said Mary, still peeking out the window. "Uuuh, Dr. Hans I need-"

She was interrupted by Maggie waving her arms and shushing her.

Mary hesitating, said, "Oh … Never mind," staring at Maggie, she said goodbye and hung up.

"What are you shushing me for?" asked Mary.

"Well … we don't want to bring it up now. We're going to surprise this asshole!"

The seriousness of the moment began to fade as Mary noticed the expression changing on Maggie's face. The two girls began reading one another's mind as they both raced for the bathroom laughing.

The Other Life of Mary Abrams | 63

Chapter 9:

The First Summit Meeting

The downstairs dining room was filled with dignitaries from all over the world. Electricity filled the air as the guests sat at breakfast and talked about the World Summit, some conversing in their own ethnic back-ground, anticipating the meetings.

Over in the corner sat Professor Hans dressed in his usual dark brown suit, white shirt, no tie with brown loafers. Glenn Taste and Bill Moss both had on dark blue jeans, expressing themselves with different styled sweaters, Moss wore his favorite, white and blue, with buttons down the middle and large pockets, trimmed in black, with school logo.

Glenn chose to wear an army green v-neck, trimmed in gold around the sleeves and bottom. Looking very collegiate, the two were no match for Larry Daniels. Slumping in his chair next to Professor Hans, Larry Daniels sat dressed in a designer Todd Snider gray and blue blend jacket with matching khaki pants accented with Cole Haan loafers. Determined not to overeat he sat quietly, his attention elsewhere. The scraps of food left on their plates and half drunk coffee showed the group had come to breakfast early.

"Man, I'm really full," said Bill Moss rubbing and patting his stomach.

The Other Life of Mary Abrams | 65

"Tell us something we don't know," said Glenn Taste. "Did you leave anything for Maggie and Mary?" Glenn asked, balling up a napkin and throwing it at Moss.

"Hey asshole your plate is empty too," exclaimed Moss, picking up the napkin and throwing it back.

"My plate is not empty Mossy! Professor Hans and I both have food on our plate."

"Okay gentlemen!" said Dr. Hans, putting down his coffee cup. Moss wanted to give him the finger but decided not to, in front of Professor Hans.

Larry Daniels, ignoring the squabble, was eyeing one of the young ladies near him. Turning around with a mischievous smile, Daniels said

"didn't you guys ever hear, man does not live by bread alone?" Changing his expression and looking green in the face, he blurted out "I think I'm going to be sick! Ooh upset stomach!"

Glenn and Bill, looking at Larry, turned to each other and started laughing.

"Hell, I didn't know Mother Teresa was on this trip, I thought it was just college students, didn't you Moss? "stated Glenn Taste.

Moss let out a loud belch and said, "Good Bible quote. Larry! Bless you my son." The two started back laughing.

"Gentlemen, gentlemen!" said Professor Hans. "The ladies should be down in a minute."

"Speaking of ladies, here comes at least one," said Glenn Taste. Mary was dressed in a conservative dark blue pantsuit with a white cotton blouse and black loafers, while Maggie wore a yellow Donna Karan silk blouse, white Neiman Marcus designer pants, and low black heels, all accented with jewelry. They worked their way through the crowds of people looking for their table. Larry turning to look, called out to the girls, "Hey Mag!

Hey Mary! Over here!"

Thinking of Glenn's comments, Larry gave Glenn an angry look that lasted forever. "Not funny! Not funny at all!" said Daniels standing up and 66 | James Edwards III

reaching into his pocket. Pulling out the keys to the van, he said, "I'm going to the bathroom and then to the van, Dr. Hans."

The Professor nodded giving his permission. After Larry left, Professor Hans turned to Bill and Glenn shaking his head with indignation.

"Hey Professor! Hey guys, where's Larry going?" Maggie said, smiling as she watched him walk away.

"He went to get the van," said Professor Hans, picking up a glass of water and taking a sip.

"Still interested, huh?" said Mary, as she began singing, *Let Me Be Your Baby Tonight.*

Maggie looked at Mary with a devilish smile. She turned her attention to the rest of her classmates. "Well what's up with everybody? You guys act like you've been to a funeral."

Feeling guilty from his comment and not wanting to look her in the face, Glenn looked off to the side and said, "Everything's cool, Mag and you know, you'll always be cool with me."

Reading between the lines of Glenn's response, she just stared at him, sensing in her heart he wasn't being truthful, as if she knew he had been talking about her.

"So, are we ready?" Mary said, bubbly with a smile.

"Aren't you young ladies eating breakfast?" asked Professor Hans.

"I'm okay," said Mary. "What about you Mag?"

Picking up a glass of orange juice off the table, Maggie turned it up and drank all of it down without stopping.

"There! That'll do me," she said, trying to get her breath.

Not expecting Maggie's behavior, Mary looked at her and rolled her eyes, letting out a sigh. "Like I said I'm … okay, Dr. Hans," Mary restated.

"Well," said Professor Hans, standing up. "The meeting starts at 11:00.

I'm sure by now Mr. Daniels is waiting for us outside in the van."

"Well let's do it," said Maggie, turning to Mary "You see what happens when you leave men unattended? Oh! Not you Professor! Just these college men."

The Other Life of Mary Abrams | 67

"What's up with you?" Mary said, smiling and taking Maggie's arm as the two started to leave the dining room.

Glenn Taste and Bill Moss stood up and followed the girls and the Professor as they made their way through the crowds of people. Moss, passing a table of breakfast rolls, reached and grabbed one as he headed to the exit.

Walking through the corridor of plush red carpet, the group reached the lobby and went out the door. The front of the hotel looked like a parking lot with black stretch limousines that looked like one long train.

"Over here!" yelled Larry Daniels, catching the eye of his classmates.

Dr. Hans and the students wove their way through the double parked limos to their rental van. Climbing in, the group buckled their seat belts.

Concerned about Larry's health, Dr. Hans asked, "Are you feeling better Mr. Daniels?"

"A lot better sir!" Larry said with some hesitation.

"Then were all set!" said Professor Hans. The college students in unison cried out, "Yeah! Go for it!" The van pulled away from the curb, slowly migrating into traffic.

68 | James Edwards III

Chapter 10:

Ambassadors John Dorn and James Dorn

The rising red solar planet competed with cotton white swollen clouds in a playground blue sky, playing peek-a-boo as it tried to warm up the day to 70°. Giving up, it came out of hiding. The rays reflected on the Capital Building like a lighthouse drawing boats to harbor. The van full of college students made its way down Pennsylvania Avenue to Constitution Street, turning left on First Street. They arrived at the Capital Building. The security patrol directed the van along with other traffic to the rear of the building where there was tourist parking. Finding a parking space not far from the rear entrance, the van pulled into it.

"Well class!" said Professor Hans, his voice filled with excitement,

"We're here!" Turning around in his seat to face the class, he said with authority, "Now! I'm asking everyone to be on their best behavior. I know you're all adults and I respect that! But you! You are my responsibility while we are on this trip. So, I am asking you to govern yourselves accordingly.

If you have any questions or concerns please address them now." He paused and waited for a response.

"No questions?" said the Professor standing up in the van. The college students had heard the speech before and found it to be just a formality.

"Okay then let's go." They began escaping the van making small talk, as they walked the 50 yards to the century-old marble stairs leading up to the historic building.

Standing at the entrance doors were Secret Service Agents with no facial expressions posed in unmovable positions, dressed in black suits, white shirts, ties and mentally clothed in a hypnotic trance as they checked ID and passes.

"Excuse me sir, may I have your ID and your pass?" asked the agent.

Professor Hans positioned himself in front of the college students and handed him a congressional stamped letter along with his driver's license. Looking stern-faced, the agent slowly read the letter. After finishing, he handed the letter and license back. Then he allowed the group to come through.

The US Capital Visitors Center was wall-to-wall exhilarated people mulling around and talking. Standing in the brightly-lit hallway leading to the House Chambers, a congressional page held a sign: *New York State College Professor Luas Hans.* Seeing the sign, Professor Hans and the college students headed his way. As they bumped and excused their way through the crowds of people they approached the page with exhilaration.

"Professor Hans?"

"Yes! New York State College."

"Welcome to the 11-Day World Summit!" said the congressional page.

"Thank you!" said the Professor.

"Please follow me; I'll take you to your seats."

The page took them through a marble-walled corridor with antique paintings of Presidents who had long been forgotten. The hallway opened up to the House Chambers filled with people from all over the world. They climbed the stairway leading to the balcony known as the gallery. They passed a *No Food No Drink* sign on their way to their seats.

The page handed the Professor an invitation to brunch with Ambassador John Dorn.

70 | James Edwards III

"The Ambassador will be expecting you after the meeting, Again welcome!" Turning and walking away, the guide started back down the steps.

The college students now in their seats, began squirming, trying to fit themselves in a comfortable position for what they assumed would be a long boring lecture.

"Anybody got any gum?" said Maggie sitting next to Mary Abrams, who was sitting next to Glenn and Professor Hans.

"Try under the chair seat!" said Glenn Taste giggling and laughing as he sat on the other side of Mary.

"F-you," said Maggie, becoming livid.

Mary turned to Maggie and did a puppy dog stare. "Come on Mag!

Don't let 'em get to you."

"I thought it was funny," said Bill Moss, sitting next to Larry.

Larry Daniels sat on Maggie's left side. Leaning forward, he asked Bill to define funny.

"Well …you know, imagine someone getting on their knees and getting gum from under the chair?"

Getting agitated and cutting him off. Larry demanded, "Who would do that?"

Picking up on the conversation, Professor Hans sitting on the aisle seat pulled out a handkerchief, blew and wiped his nose. He looked down the aisle at his students and shook his head with an almost smile.

"That ain't funny," said Larry. "It's gross.! Like the breakfast I had!"

The Professor, seeing the Speaker of the House come to the podium, shushed them.

"Greetings and welcome to the 11-Day World Summit," said the 50-ish gray haired short and stocky Secretary of State, wearing a matching gray suit, white shirt and red tie. Behind him sat 11 Ambassadors from around the world except for US Ambassador John Dorn.

"It is my great pleasure to introduce our own from the United States Ambassador John Dorn."

The Other Life of Mary Abrams | 71

Standing 6'2, he looked impeccable, with greyish-black hair and an athletic frame, dressed in a black suit, with white shirt, accented by a lime green tie. The *Ambassador* stood up and walked to the podium.

"Greetings my World Brothers and Sisters!" said Ambassador John Dorn. "I greet you in the name of the United States. It's my great pleasure to welcome our speakers from around the world including my brother, to the 11-Day World Summit."

His greetings caused a thunderous applause that motivated some people to stand.

Putting his notes in order, he said with a baritone voice, "I will be speaking to you about the world food crisis." The college students turned and looked directly at Bill Moss and began smiling. Looking back and frowning, Moss gave them his famous finger gesture.

"In 2013 the United Nations warned us about global grain reserves being critically low. Extreme weather means no stability. It appears that the increasing use of bio fuels has drastically changed our weather conditions.

Failed harvests in the US, Ukraine and other countries have eroded the food reserves. This year for the sixth time in 11 years, the world will need more food than it produces. And when the demand is more than the supply, you know what happens? The price of food goes up. From 2006 to 2008

the average world price for rice rose 217%; wheat rose 136%; maize 125%; and soybeans 107%. So, you can see how serious this matter is."

Picking up a glass of water sitting on the podium, he took a sip and continued.

"For the benefit of mankind we must address these issues!" Looking at his watch, he said. "I wish I had more time but I don't. So! I will govern myself accordingly. My brother Ambassador James Dorn from Canada will finish the subject. Ambassador James Dorn stood up and walked toward his brother at the podium; shaking his hand and hugging him, he turned to the people and adjusted the microphone. The audience began standing and clapping for the 6'2 ambassador brothers.

72 | James Edwards III

"Thank you world brothers and sisters," said Ambassador James Dorn, looking like his brother, dressed in a dark blue suit white shirt and orange tie. I say as my brother said: welcome! Like my brother was saying, we have a very serious food crisis! Seventy-four days is all that stands between us and starvation. That's how low food reserves have gotten. If we miss one harvest, we would all began to starve to death."

Pausing, he said with conviction, "There is a great need for genetically-altered crop seeds. Scientists are working around the clock, seven days a week to remedy this situation. There are skeptics who believe genetically-altered food is not good for the human species, but at this point what choice do we have? The research on genetically manufactured food is in its infancy. So, we will cross that bridge when we get to it."

Feeling the vibration of his cell phone in his suit pocket, he knew his time was up. "This is where we will stop today! I thank you all for coming and will see you tomorrow. May God's peace and blessings rest upon you and our planet."

Some people cheering and applauding began to make their way down front to greet and shake the hands of the Ambassadors.

"Well," said the Professor showing his age as he struggled to get up out of his seat.

"Excuse me!" said the congressional page, appearing out of nowhere.

Ambassador Dorn sent me to escort you to the luncheon.

"Thank you, young man," said Professor Hans. Turning around to his class, he motioned them to follow him and the Guide.

He took them back through the marble floor corridor to the Capital Visitors Center. He led them down a short hallway to a room with red ma-hogany French doors. Inside were hundreds of people who were given special invitations for brunch. After working his way around luncheon tables and groups of people, they arrived at their table.

"Here we are!" said the page, waiting for the group to take their seats.

"Ambassador Dorn will be with you shortly. Is there anything I can get you?" asked the page.

The Other Life of Mary Abrams | 73

Shaking his head and smiling the Professor spoke for the group.

"We're fine, young man." Acknowledging Dr. Hans, the page did a slight bow and left.

"So, where's the menu?" asked Bill Moss.

"Nothing but silverware, napkins, water, and coffee," blurted Glenn Taste.

Mary Abrams said in a sing-song voice: "Don't forget the candles."

"Yeah!" said Maggie sitting next to Larry Daniels. "Nice table setting but I'm with Bill on this one. What are we havin'?" Noticing Larry's expression, she asked. "What's wrong with you?"

"Just not feeling good,. My stomach is still upset from breakfast. I think I'll find a bathroom." Before anyone could respond, Larry jumped up from the table on his way to the rest room.

"Well," said Professor Hans, "I hope it's nothing serious like a kidn-"

The Professor's voice was drowned out by the commotion of the 11

Ambassadors entering the room and hundreds of people clapping, whistling and cheering as they are caught up in the moment. After shaking several hands, Ambassador John Dorn went over to his guest table. He greeted them all one by one before he took his seat.

"I know I met you all on the plane but it's good to see you in the light of day. I hope all of you are being well taken care of." He directed his attention to Professor Hans. Ambassador Dorn said,"I believe you have my number Dr. Hans?" asked Ambassador Dorn.

"Most certainly," said the Professor, smiling.

Maggie and Mary couldn't wait to ask him about his aid, Samuel Moore. But before they could get into the matter, the waitress came with an array of food choices: steak, chicken and seafood.

"We have several cuisines May I serve you?" asked the waitress.

"Aaaa. This looks good," said Ambassador Dorn as he chose the seafood platter. "Tell me Dr. Hans, how long have you been teaching?"

Interrupting the question Bill Moss hollered out, "I'll take two steaks."

Everyone at the table turned and looked at him.

Filling intimidated by stares, he blurted out. "One is for Larry! Remember he went to the rest room?" Smiling and patting Moss on the back, Maggie turned to Mary and asked, "What are you having?"

"Chicken's good," said Mary, winking at Moss to console him.

"You must've read my mind," said Maggie laying out her silverware.

"Roasted chicken."

"Same here!" said Glenn Taste, unfolding his napkin.

"I apologize for my students," said Professor Hans,"You were saying?"

Ambassador Dorn restated his question. "How long have you been teaching?"

Taking the chicken platter the Professor responded with pride, "Close to 40 years."

The chit-chat continued as the time began to fly by. Ambassador Dorn, eating the last of his shrimp said, "That was a great meal!" Wiping his mouth with a napkin, he looked at Mary and smiled.

Maggie asked rudely, "Do you have an African American aid name Samuel Moore?"

"Maggie!" said Professor Hans. "Mind your manners!"

"No, it's okay," said Ambassador Dorn, "Yes I do."

"Well he's been following us since we left New York."

"Yeah … somethin' … like that," Mary said, feeling some anxiety. "He seems to be everywhere we go!"

"Are you sure?" said the Ambassador, looking very concerned.

"I heard his voice!" injected Bill Moss stuttering, "in in the men's room."

Cutting off his conversation, the Ambassador said, "He is a man, a very important one.

I think there might be some mistaken identity. I sent Mr. Moore home yesterday."

The college kids looked puzzled looking at one another. They could not believe what they were hearing.

The Other Life of Mary Abrams | 75

"Yesterday," Mary and Maggie said in unison. Reaching in her purse, Maggie pulled out her cell phone. Turning on the video, she passed the phone to the Ambassador Dorn. "Looked at this!" she said. "he ran by our hotel this morning."

Ambassador Dorn took the cell phone and watched the video.

"Looks like a bunch of guys in great shape to me." He said with a mysterious smile, passing the phone back to her.

Maggie rewinded the video while Mary looked on, mystified at what they saw.

"This can't be Mag," said Mary shaking, "Where's Moore?"

Maggie speechless, responded. "I don't know … He was on the video jogging! You and I both saw him!" Her voice ended abruptly.

"Yeah this guy's a nuisance," chimed in Taste and Moss, supporting their classmates.

The girls, emotionally upset, decided to go to the restroom. Leaving the table, Maggie put her arm around Mary as they pushed their way through the crowd.

"You know he's lying about sending him home Mag! We both saw him.

How could someone just disappear off of a video?"

Comforting Mary as they approached the restrooms, they saw Larry Daniels talking to a female food server.

"Upset stomach, huh?" Maggie announced with condemnation.

Daniels, standing with his back to Maggie, heard her voice, he nervously said goodbye to the waitress and then turned around. "Hey Mag, hey Mary."

Ignoring him, they pushed past him to the restroom. Coming out ten minutes later, Larry was waiting for them.

"You ladies looking for an escort?" asked Daniels jokingly.

Giving him a "you're full of shit" look, Mary and Maggie remained silent as they walked back to their table with Larry in tow.

"Is everything okay?" said Professor Hans, looking at the three of them. Hesitating, Maggie said a long "Yeah …"

76 | James Edwards III

"I assure you, we will get to the bottom of this," said the Professor.

Mary and Maggie nodded.

Turning his attention back to Glenn and Bill, he picked up his program and said.

"How about you guys?"

"Cool as ice," said Glenn Taste.

"Yeah," said Moss, seconding. "Cool as ice."

Remembering Larry's steak, Moss said. "Oh, yeah Larry, I got you a steak and all the trimmings sitting right here next to me."

"Where?" asked Larry, tucking in his shirt.

"In the chair!" Moss said as he lifted the plate.

"I'm not eating any food sitting in a chair! Where people's butts have been," Larry said dramatically. "And besides my stomach is just settling.

No way. I ain't eating nothing. " Larry said shaking his finger at Moss.

"That's enough" said Professor Hans. "I'm sorry you didn't get a chance to meet Ambassador Dorn, Mr. Daniels. I think you would've liked him."

"Yeah I'm sorry about that Professor. I would have loved to have formally met him. "

"Well," sighed Professor Hans, "if there is nothing else, shall we go?"

Dr. Hans led the students around dignitaries shaking hands and hugging one another to the exit door, down the marble steps out into the parking lot to the Rental. Climbing in they all buckled up and were off. The noise of the tires on the pavement was the only sound heard. No one spoke.

Arriving at the hotel and parking, they unloaded and went inside. Catching the elevator to their floor they all said goodnight, see you in the morning and went to their prospective rooms.

The Other Life of Mary Abrams | 77

Chapter 11:

Ambassadors Thaddeus Ivanoff and Thomas Salinger Cloudy skies came with the morning, blocking the sun, as cold boisterous wind coming out of the Gulf of Mexico caused leaves to blow excessively, twirling and windmilling across the manicured lawns that were always im-maculate for tourists. The howling of the wind and forces against the window pane of the Hey Adams Hotel, awakened Glenn Taste out of his dream.

" Noooo!" he said, kicking in his sleep, waking up Bill Moss.

"Hey … What's going on?" asked Moss sitting up rubbing his eyes.

"Oh! Bro, I just had the craziest dream! " Glenn said climbing out of his cot and picking up his book bag. Taking out some papers, he walked over to the table and sat down.

"What kind a dream?" Moss asked, not really interested, sitting on the side of the bed.

Still looking at his astrology charts Glenn said. "I dreamed that we were surrounded by all these guys and they were dressed in …"

" Hey you two! Shut the fuck up, " said Larry Daniels, putting a pillow over his head.

Looking startled that Larry, was awake, Glenn vocalized: "Hey Bro this is serious stuff! With all the shit that's been going on, there has to be some explanation. Remember! I'm the one that went blind on the plane."

The Other Life of Mary Abrams | 79

After calming down, he picked up a pencil and drew a line on the chart.

Dismissing Larry's comments, Glenn began talking to himself.

"Venus and Jupiter are pinpointing a planetary conjunction which appeared in the sky thousands of years ago in the constellation of Leo. All the data point to June 17."

Daniels, sitting up in bed, looked at Moss and asked, "What the hell is he talking about?"

Moss shrugging his shoulders exclaimed, "Hell, if I know. I'm gonna go shower. I'm ready for breakfast." Getting up he headed for the bathroom.

"Breakfast? I believe there's some leftover pizza on the counter," Larry said with a devilish smile.

"Where?" asked Moss, as he walked to the counter looking.

Waiting for his chance, Larry grabbed a shirt and a fresh pair of jeans and darted to the bathroom laughing. Realizing that he had been fooled, Moss ran toward the door but Larry closed and locked it.

"You're a fucking asshole Larry!" cried Moss, as he banged on the door.

"You don't know him by now, bro.," interjected Glenn, not looking up but still studying his astrology charts.

"That's the problem: I've known him too long," Moss yelled walking away from the restroom door. Pulling a chair out from the table, he sat next to Glenn.

"You really believe in this stuff?" asked Moss, becoming curious.

Breaking his concentration, Glenn looked up at him and smiled. "You gotta believe in something bro."

"Yeah … I guess so," said Moss, digging in his nose and thinking about his father's hamburger business. His father was determined to make it work, although his mom was against his dad investing the life savings. His father's gut feeling was right. Paying off, they had a successful business.

Fifteen minutes later, Larry emerged from the bathroom.

"Next!" said Daniels, boasting as he zipped up his jeans and put on his socks and shoes.

80 | James Edwards III

Turning red as he stared at Larry, Moss picked up his clothes off the bed and headed for the bathroom. Reaching the door, he turned around and said, "Hey Larry that wasn't cool, asshole!"

Standing there smiling mischievously Larry, didn't respond.

Moss raising both of his index fingers, causing his clothes to fall on the floor. Bending over and picking them up he said "put a shirt on jerk."

Moss turned around and slammed the bathroom door.

Ignoring Moss' display of anger, Larry said to Glenn. "Hey man I'll be downstairs." Putting his royal blue collarless shirt on, He walked out the door.

As Larry made his way downstairs to the lobby, Professor Hans, Mary, and Maggie were coming out of the dining room.

"Good morning," said Professor Hans. "Where's the rest of the gang?"

"Oh … They'll be down soon," said Larry looking at Maggie.

"Well I hope they're not too much longer. We're running a little late."

As Professor Hans was speaking, the two missing classmates arrived.

"Good morning, " said the Professor, looking over his glasses.

"Morning," said Glenn and Bill, nodding at Maggie and Mary, while ignoring Larry Daniels.

"You guys grab some breakfast," said Professor Hans, taking the keys from Daniels. "We'll go get the van and you can meet us out front."

Realizing that they were running late, the two of them, said "okay" as they hurried into the dining room.

Twenty minutes later, the guys were standing in front of the hotel waiting for the Professor and their classmates. Finishing an egg and cheese bagel, Bill Moss said, "Here they come!" The van pulled up and they hurried up and got in. The drive was déjà vu of the day before down Pennsylvania Avenue to Constitution Street, left on first. They arrived. Exiting the van, they walked to the Capitol's marble steps where there were lines of people waiting to clear security. Making it through security, they were greeted by a familiar face, the Congressional page of Ambassador John The Other Life of Mary Abrams | 81

Dorn. He escorted them to their seats, through the hallway, to the steps leading to the gallery, passed the *No Eating rf Drinking* sign to their row.

Entering Row 21 the young college kids fell into their seats.

"Greetings … citizens of the world," said the speaker of the house. "I would like to introduce you to a friend of mine and a friend of yours: world business leader Thaddeus Ivanoff from Russia."

Thunderous applause and clapping brought up to the podium a 6'2

stone-faced man with hair like Albert Einstein. And an off-white suit with a powder blue shirt and polyester grey tie.

"Greetings world brothers and sisters! I greet you in the name of Russia. Our topic today is the planet's resources. Energy … the force that drives the world. When I was a young man, I owned a motorcycle. I was not aware of the energy that powered my machine nor that there was a limited amount. The three largest-producing oil countries in the world are Venezuela, Saudi Arabia and Canada. Together combined they produce over 20,000 barrels of oil a day. You might ask yourself: where is all the oil going? Well, industry consumes a percentage but the majority of consumption is by the recreation of commuting back and forth, These three countries alone have oil reserves in the billions but how long will they last at our present-day consumption? I hope I've given you something to think about! I will now let my colleague Ambassador Thomas Salinger of China complete the second half of our program."

The audience gave a standing ovation while the two Ambassadors shook hands and hugged.

"Greetings my brothers and sisters of the world! It is a great honor to speak to you today. The excessive consumption of fossil fuel can be resolved by alternate energy sources. For instance, solar energy is an unde-veloped technology that can save us all."

Applause broke out throughout the room. The college students took their cue from the Professor; they clapped when he clapped.

"How much longer?" asked Glenn Taste, sitting next to Larry Daniels.

82 | James Edwards III

"Who knows?" mumbled Larry. "Hey Moss, what time is it?" asked Daniels.

Moss pulled out a half-eaten danish stuck to his phone. Taking a bite, he said. " It's 2:00."

Just as Mary and Maggie started to shush them, there appeared a 6'4, 350-pound usher, pointing at Bill Moss.

"You, yes! You, Come with me! There is no eating or drinking. Didn't you see the sign?" yelled the usher, competing with the noise of the audience.

Feeling like a high school student who got caught cheating on a final exam. Moss, red-faced and embarrassed, slowly got up, while Professor Hans and his classmates looked on with expressions of bewilderment. The usher escorted Moss down the carpeted stairs to the first floor, back through the pictured hallway of presidents to the reception center.

"When you finish that young man, you can return to your seat," said the usher as he gave Moss a misbehaving stare. Turning and walking away, he disappeared among the crowd. The embarrassment began to subside as Bill pulled out the danish and finished eating it. Having messy hands, he headed for the bathroom. Finding it, he took a leak and washed his hands.

As he was coming out, not paying attention, he bumped into an elderly woman knocking her papers out of her hand.

"I'm so sorry ma'am I didn't see you," Moss said, bending over and picking up her papers. Noticing an invitation from Ambassador John Dorn, he asked, "Are you a guest of Ambassador John Dorn?"

"No, I'm not!" said the elderly woman nervously.

"Well … I just noticed his name on your invitation, " Moss said, explaining as he handed back her papers.

"Oh … I see!" said the older woman angrily. "Well that's not mine young man; it belongs to someone else."

Starting to chuckle, Bill realized she was serious. Looking closer at the senior citizen, he realized she looked familiar to him.

"Do I know you?" asked Moss, staring rudely.

The Other Life of Mary Abrams | 83

"I don't think so," said the elderly woman, covering up her name tag on her blouse.

"Oh well … Maybe not," Moss said. Studying her facial features, he thought to himself, *this has to be the handicapped lady on the plane that couldn't walk.*

Interrupting his thoughts, without expression she said, "Well … It was nice meeting you. Have a nice day." She half smiled and walked away.

I know that's her! Moss thought to himself. *Wait till I tell the gang!*

He made his way back through crowds of people, down the pictured hallway to the blue carpeted stairs of the gallery. Climbing the final set of stairs, he could hear the applause signaling that the meeting was over. Reaching Professor Hans and his classmates, he couldn't wait to tell them.

"Oh, I see you're back," said Professor Hans.

"Yeah," Moss said, feeling ashamed, while his classmates poked fun at him.

"Okay," said Professor Hans. "That's enough."

He led the college students through the maze of people down the steps through the hallway to the parking lot. They loaded up the van and drove the short distance back to the hotel. Bill Moss could hardly contain himself on the ride back.

As the college students entered the lobby behind Professor Hans, Moss whispered to Mary and Maggie to meet him upstairs with the rest of the guys. He had something important to tell them. Looking curious, the young ladies said, "Give us an hour."

An hour later the girls were knocking on the door. Opening the door, Larry Daniels invited them in. Happy to see Maggie, he said, "Welcome, ladies, to our humble abode!"

Moving clothes out of the way, Mary and Maggie found a place to sit.

"All right, what's this about?" asked Mary and Maggie, as the guys pulled up chairs, making a half circle in front of them.

84 | James Edwards III

Having revealed some details to Glenn and Larry before the girls got there, Bill Moss verbally exploded.

"I know you guys remember the elderly woman on the plane?" Moss said excitedly.

"The one they made such a fuss over during the storm?" said Mary.

"Yes, I remember."

Maggie nodded in agreement.

"Well … Guess what?" cried Moss. "I ran into her in the hall and she could walk!"

Maggie and Mary were somewhat bewildered. "Go on!" They said, becoming more interested.

"Well … guess what?"

"You already said that, bro," said Glenn Taste, braiding the loose end of his honest ponytail.

"Cut the bull shit, Mossy!" Larry said running out of patience. "Get to the point!"

Moss, too excited to give Larry his traditional finger gesture, continued.

"See, I was coming out of the bathroom."

" Bathroom?" said Mary. "Oh no, Not the bathroom again."

"No! I'm serious. This was the same lady that was on the plane and guess what? She was a guest of Ambassador John Dorn."

"And?" said the group.

"Don't you see?" said Moss, barely containing himself. All this must be tied together: Glenn going blind on the plane, the lady being able to walk, the Boy Scout with the limp, Samuel Moore not showing up on the video. There has to be a connection!"

His classmates listening intensely and began to agree with him.

"Bill's right," said Maggie. "Maybe we should discuss this with the Professor."

"Naw," said Larry Daniels, "He'll thinks we're just a bunch of crazy college kids."

The Other Life of Mary Abrams | 85

Did you get her name?" asked Glenn.

"No," said Moss, wiping the sweat from his fore head with his sleeve.

"She covered it up."

"Covered what up?" asked Mary, leaning forward.

"Her name tag," said Moss, demonstrating.

"Mmm … That's strange," said Maggie. "Why would she do that.?"

"She doesn't want us to know who she is 'cause, she's connected to Ambassador Dorn and Moore," Bill said, trying to explain while using hand gestures.

"Hey bro," asked Glenn, "didn't you videotape the Ambassador coming down the aisle?"

All eyes on Larry, he said,"I don't remember."

"Well … just check your phone, butt hole! It's got to be there," said Bill aggressively staring at Larry.

Squinting at Bill with piercing blue eyes, Larry took out his cell phone and searched for the video. Finding it, he laid the phone on the table so they all could see.

"Okay," said Maggie. "There's Professor Hans and the Ambassador is behind him."

As Ambassador John Dorn was coming into view the lights went out on the plane.

"Aww," said the college students with disappointment. " You can't see him."

"Hey!" exclaimed Glenn Taste. "When the ball of light hit us the power came back on. "

"Quiet!" said Mary. "Listen!"

As the students quieted down and focused on the audio, they heard the captain ask, "Can you tell us your name?"

"Margaret Walker," said the elderly woman. The college kids raised their arms in the air and gave a victory cheer.

"So, what …" said Larry. "We know her name."

86 | James Edwards III

"Don't you see," said Moss, continuing his excitement. "Now that we have her name and the name of the Boy Scout we can look them up. Maybe they can tell us what's going on. Margaret Walker couldn't walk when she got *on* the plane but now she can. The Boy Scout limped when he went on stage. But didn't when he climbed on the bus."

"Look her up for that? " said Larry. "What's that got to do with Dorn and Moore?"

"I don't know," said Bill. "She's Dorn's guest like we are. It wouldn't hurt."

Mary and Maggie began yawning as the hour drifted into the night.

Agreeing with Bill Moss, they made a pact to find out the connection if any, to Ambassador John Dorn. Calling it a night, they said *see you in the morning* in college fashion: hugging one another and slapping each other's hands.

Leaving the guys' room, Mary and Maggie walked down the hall talking in a whisper while Larry Daniels stood in the threshold watching them.

Reaching their hotel room, they slid their card in the door.

"Good night ladies," Daniels hollered down the hall. Getting no response, he closed the door.

The Other Life of Mary Abrams | 87

Chapter 11:

Ambassadors Philip Perez and Matthew Isser

A bright orange sun and a crystal blue sky created a beautiful fall morning.

From the north came a flock of geese that flew over the Hey-Adams hotel heading south for the winter. In the quietness of the early hours you could hear Professor Hans snoring. Hearing his cell phone melody, he awakened out of his sleep.

"Hello … Dr. Hans how are you?" said the voice on the other end.

"I'm doing okay," he said, recognizing the voice.

"I hope it isn't too early? I had some time so I thought I would call you."

"I appreciate that, Dr. Hunter!" said Professor Hans, putting on his glasses.

"So … How are the dreams?" said Dr. Hunter, clearing his throat.

"Well," said the Professor, "they're not as frequent."

"That's good!" said the psychiatrist. "And your last dream?"

After a long sigh, Dr. Hans said, "I dreamed I was walking down a dusty road. It looked as though I was in a desert. I remember hills or moun-tains on each side. A huge bright sun in the sky. All of a sudden, I heard a voice. When I turned around to look, I couldn't see anybody."

"And what did the voice say?" asked Dr. Hunter, taking notes.

The Other Life of Mary Abrams | 89

"I'm not sure! It sounded like a foreign language. My gut feeling tells me the voice is trying to tell me something or direct me somewhere, you know, like a destination."

"Mmm … tell me, Dr. Hans, was the voice male or female?"

"The strange thing about that …is … I can't tell."

The psychiatrist, thinking of a previous session, said "I think we're making some progress. I'm looking forward to seeing you when you get back."

"Thank you, Dr. Hunter. I appreciate your time and your concern."

"You're welcome! Enjoy the rest of your trip. Goodbye!"

Hanging up, Professor Hans sat on the side of the bed thinking about what he considered nightmares instead of dreams. Hearing, his cell phone ringing, he thought, *now what?*

"Hello …"

"Professor Hans! Are you okay?" asked Mary Abrams, panicky.

"Yes … I'm fine. What's wrong?"

"Oh, nothing's wrong. We were wondering why you weren't at breakfast?"

"Breakfast? What time is it?" said Professor Hans, looking for his watch.

"It's 9:30," Mary said trying not to giggle.

"My Lord! I've overslept! Listen, when all of you are finished eating.

Go ahead and get the van and I'll meet you out front. I'm gonna take a quick shower."

"Okay Professor Hans, see you in a minute," said Mary.

"So, what did he say?" asked Larry Daniels, setting down his glass of orange juice.

"He said for us to finish up. And go get the van and he would meet us out front."

"Cool!" said Larry, getting up from the table, putting on his sunglasses.

"Yeah I'm finished," said Maggie Werks.

"Me too," said Glenn. "What about you Moss?"

90 | James Edwards III

Chewing up the last of his egg omelet, Bill nodded while putting a chocolate doughnut in his jacket.

Larry popped Moss on the back of the head. "That's enough, let's go."

Moss slowly got up from the table, rubbing his head. Drinking the last of his large orange juice, he followed his classmates out the door. After retrieving the van, the students drove to the front of the hotel and waited.

"Hey, when you guys wanta find this Margaret Walker?" asked Maggie, thinking about her biological parents, wondering if she would ever find them. Although she loved her foster parents she often thought of her real mother and father.

"You guys still on that?" said Larry Daniels, sitting behind the wheel.

"Yes, we are Larry," Mary shrieked.

"Hey, calm down!" said Larry. Dr. Hans is coming, Larry unlocked the door. As the Professor was showing his age getting in the van, Maggie whispered, "Let's try tomorrow tonight."

Agreeing silently Bill, Glenn and Mary nodded, while Larry stared at them. The Professor closed the door and buckled up. Daniels pulled away from the curb and started down the red brick horseshoe driveway leading into traffic. Down Pennsylvania Avenue to Constitution Street turning left on First Street, they reached the capital building. Parking next to a news truck, they unbuckled their seatbelts and climbed out of the van. Walking the short distance, they entered the noisy US capital visitor center and saw their page. He greeted them and took them to their seats.

The speaker of the house, dressed in a black suit, white shirt and black tie, greeted the people. "We, the United States, welcome you to the 11th Day World Summit. Our two speakers today will be Ambassadors Philip Perez of Argentina and Matthew Isser of Algeria. Ambassador Perez will take the podium first."

Approaching the podium Ambassador Perez yelled out, "Diso es bueno"

Thunderous applause resounded from a small section of the audience signifying that there were a high attendance of Spanish speaking people.

The Other Life of Mary Abrams | 91

"Thank you! Thank you! Greetings my World Brothers and Sisters. I greet you in the name of my country, Argentina," said the 6'2 Ambassador, dressed in a dark gray suit, white shirt and red tie.

"My topic this morning will be on World Pollution … World pollution has continued to rise since the Great Famine and Black Death ended in 1350. There are more people being born than there are dying; therefore, the world is being overcrowded. The waste that human beings are creating from our technologies and plain body waste is destroying our planet. The poorer nations are suffering the most; Khoramabad in Iran, Kabul in Afghanistan and Ralpur in India are just a few of the worst cities in the world. The dangers of pollution are threatening our way of life. We can no longer ignore this problem!"

Interrupted by applause, the Ambassador waited until the noise died down and said. "I thank you for your time. My colleague Ambassador Isser will elaborate further. Again, thank you."

Applauding again, they continued until Ambassador Matthew Isser walked to the podium.

"Thank you," said Ambassador Isser standing 6 '2, dressed in a tan two button suit, white shirt and green tie. "Greetings my World Brothers and Sisters! I greet you in the name of my country Algeria. As Ambassador Perez was saying, we must address this issue now! Air pollution has reached a critical point. The burning of fossil fuel produces massive amounts of carbon dioxide and sulfur dioxide in the air. How can we breathe or live in a toxic environment? Inventions that make our lives easier should not destroy us."

People begin to applaud and stand. The Ambassador continued for another 45 minutes and then ended his lecture to the applause and sound of jubilation coming from the throngs of people.

The college professor and the students began exiting the auditorium, following one another in line like kindergartners going to the playground.

They reached the van and climbed in; buckling up they were on their way.

92 | James Edwards III

Twenty minutes later they arrived at the Hey-Adams Hotel. Finding a parking space, they unloaded and went into the hotel. Getting on the elevator Professor Hans asked with a half smile "Are you kids enjoying yourselves?"

The responses were: *the capital's cool, yeah, I'm getting knowledge, everything's cool, they love to talk.* They reached their hotel floor. Exiting the elevator, they said good night to the Professor.

"You guys want to come to our room?" asked Mary and Maggie. Agreeing, they followed the young coeds to their room. As Maggie opened the door, the guys rushed in to find the most comfortable piece of furniture.

Throwing her key card on the table Maggie said, "Here you go." She handed Bill Moss her laptop computer.

"And don't look for no sloppy Joe restaurants," Larry said grinning.

"Larry … please!" said Mary in a serious tone, as she put her purse on the table.

Moss raised his left index finger, while typing with his right, never looked up.

"What website are you using?" asked Glenn.

"Citizen search!" exclaimed Moss.

"Why don't you try find the bastard.com."

Maggie and Mary, getting chips and pop for refreshments turned around to look at Glenn.

Looking up, Bill said laughing, "There ain't no such website."

Noticing that Glenn was displaying an *I'm telling you the truth* look, Moss said in a whisper, "Are you serious?"

Glenn, staring with no expression, began a slow-motion smile.

Moss was startled back to his search by an audible ping on the computer. Looking at the screen, he said, "I got it, you won't believe it! Margaret Walker, 19515 Mary Street, Hagerstown in Maryland. It's only 22

miles away."

Looking at each other with astonishment. Larry said, "It's just coincidence!"

The Other Life of Mary Abrams | 93

"Whether it is or not," said Mary, "we're still going."

The rest of her classmates, excluding Larry, walked over to her and said, "We're with you."

Maggie, patting Mary on the back, said, "It was just a coincidence, Mary Street."

Having accomplished their goal, Bill, Larry, and Glenn said goodnight.

As they left, they mulled over the day's events. Walking four doors down to their hotel room, they entered …and crashed for the night.

94 | James Edwards III

Chapter 12:

Ambassadors Andrew Cresas and Simon Lubin

The morning that followed, the sun stubbornly refuse to shine. Blocking the sun's rays were dark gray storm clouds that released the water that had been drawn up from previous warm days.

"This is 98.1 WASH– FM. Our weather report for this morning: spot-ted showers on and off throughout the day. So, take an umbrella along."

"Did I bring an umbrella?" Mary thought to herself, listening to the radio. She finished brushing her teeth and left the bathroom. Walking over to her suitcase, she unzipped it and began rustling through her belongings.

Hearing all the noise, Maggie woke up.

"Hey Mary," said Maggie yawning and stretching.

"Good morning!" smiled Mary.

"Good as any, I guess!" Maggie said. Sitting up in bed in a Buddha position, picking up a brush off the dresser she asked, "What do you think?"

Mary walked over to the bed across from Maggie and sat down, putting on her blouse she said. "About what...?"

"Well … you know, going to see Margaret Walker to see if she has any connection to Ambassador Dorn and Samuel Moore."

Putting on her shoes Mary said. "It's all bizarre to me. I got a black guy following me. Whispering 'Mary' to everybody but me! We videotaped The Other Life of Mary Abrams | 95

this clown for evidence and he doesn't show up on the video … then a Boy Scout who had a limp when he walked on stage. But when he comes off, no limp? Go figure."

"Yeah … Don't forget about Glenn going blind on the plane and then getting a phone call from the hotel lobby. After the call, he can see again cra-zy."

"Yeah that was crazy and you know, Mag, what's even crazier?"

Maggie, looking inquisitive, asked, "What's that?"

"I saw the ball of light too!"

"Get out of here … Well, you didn't go blind?"

"Why I didn't, I don't know but I could feel the energy. It felt like electricity moving through me. I could see my life like a movie. The part that seemed strange was my mother was holding me but she didn't look like my mother. You know what I'm trying to say?"

"Wow," said Maggie with raised eyebrows, " that doesn't make any sense.

Hey …you think the light had something to do with Margaret Walker?"

Shaking her head Mary said, "I … don't … know? We're only going by what Bill told us … Why would Margaret Walker lie and say she wasn't a guest of John Dorn? And then cover up her name tag. Why would Ambassador John Dorn lie and say he sent his aide, Samuel Moore, home when you and I saw him jogging. Who are these people? What do they want? Who am I? That someone would keep following me?" Mary said getting upset. "People need to be who they say they are."

Maggie stood up and walked over to Mary and sat down next to her.

Putting her arm around Mary, she said in a soft whisper, "Mary, it'll be okay. The summit is almost over and we can get the hell out of this city."

In a soft whimper, Mary said, "Thanks Mag, for caring."

Ping! Came from the window. There was a short interval and they heard the noise again. *Ping!*

Mary asked, "What was that?" becoming frightened.

"I don't know," said Maggie getting up and going over to the window.

Looking up at her were her classmates. Maggie opened the window.

96 | James Edwards III

"What the hell you guys doing? Trying to break the window?"

With cupped hands to his mouth, Daniels yelled, "We're having breakfast on the veranda!"

"O-kay! We'll be down." Maggie yelled back, closing the window.

Maggie grabbed her clothes off the bed and headed to the bathroom. "I'll be out in a minute, Mary!" said Maggie closing the bathroom door. After putting on her shoes, Mary stood up and walked over to the window. Looking out, she saw a black SUV pull up and an African-American man in a black suit exit, headed for the hotel lobby.

That's him … Mary thought! *Samuel Moore!* Mary grabbed her purse, umbrella and jacket and ran out of the room. Getting down to the lobby she frantically looked for the stranger. *There he is!* Rushing to catch up to the 6'1 African American man, she tripped and fell. Hearing the commotion behind him, he turned around, walked over to her and helped her up.

Realizing it wasn't Samuel Moore Mary felt embarrassed and foolish.

"Are you all right?" asked the good-looking African-American man.

Blushing, Mary said, "Yes, thank you. I must've tripped."

"Well, it happens to the best of us," said the man.

"Do I know you? You look familiar," asked Mary. Before the stranger could answer Maggie showed up.

"Oh my God! It's *Edward J!* " said Maggie pushing her hair back and getting excited and giddy.

Realizing that this was the famous R&B soul singer, Mary connected his familiarity to his being a celebrity.

"Is there a problem here?" said the concierge.

"Not at all," said the two female college students, smiling from ear to ear.

"Can I have a picture with you?" asked Maggie pushing back her cop-per-colored red hair.

Without answering, the R&B singer moved into position with the young college students. After Maggie took the picture of the three of them, the soul singer shook Mary's hand and gave Maggie a hug.

The Other Life of Mary Abrams | 97

"Ladies, have a nice day," he said then walked away with the concierge.

"Do you believe that Mary? *Edward J the singer* … Wow! Doesn't get any better than that."

"Yeah … He was quite handsome. For a minute, I forgot why I even came down here." Shaking her head in frustration, Mary exclaimed, "I thought he was *Samuel Moore*!"

Glenn Taste, coming from outside, seeing the girls in the lobby, called to them, "Hey ladies we're eating out on the veranda. It stopped raining."

The two young coeds, still talking about the singer, followed Glenn out to the covered patio.

"Good morning ladies," said Professor Hans, adjusting his glasses.

"Good morning Dr. Hans!" said Mary and Maggie, ignoring Larry.

"Morning, ladies!" said Daniels flirtatiously.

Mumbling good morning to Larry, the female students sat down.

"You ladies grab something to eat," said the professor, "Mr. Moss went to gas up the van and should be back in a half hour."

The two young coeds found the menu and ordered breakfast. By the time Bill Moss got back they were finished.

Entering the patio, Bill announced, "Hey everybody. I'm back. We're all set, gassed up and ready to go." Bill spoke in between eating a bag of potato chips.

Standing up, the Professor led the group out to the van. Bill Moss climbed in the driver's seat and drove them to the capital building. By now, they were accustomed to the congressional page greeting them and taking them to their seats.

Dressed in a dark green suit, white shirt and tie the speaker of the house addressed the people.

"We the United States welcome you to the 11 Day World Summit.

Today's guest speakers will be Ambassadors Andrew Creses and Simon Lubin."

Ambassador Creses took the podium first, receiving a thunderous applause.

98 | James Edwards III

"Thank you … thank you. Greetings my world brothers and sisters."

said the 6'1 Ambassador dressed in a gray pinstriped suit, white shirt and pink tie. "I greet you in the name of my country Kazakhstan! Today's topic is world terrorism. Terrorism is based on an individual's ideology! His mindset … as to how he sees the world. Influence of a good cultural environment will keep most people from getting involved in terrorist organizations. There must be laws in place that are fair to all individuals regardless of their gender, race or color. Most people respond in violence when they feel they have been mistreated and the powers that be will not listen to them. All violence begins in the mind, according to UNESCO, an organization that keeps track of world violence."

Taking out a handkerchief and wiping his forehead, the Ambassador said, "Remember, terrorism is an ideology that must be replaced with new thinking, again I thank you … It seems my time has come to an end, so I ask you to greet and welcome Ambassador Simon Lubin."

Ambassador Lubin stood up and walked to the platform smiling and shaking hands with Ambassador Creses. Lubin, 6'1, wearing a navy-blue suit with a white shirt and purple tie, held up his hand in a peace sign.

"Greetings my world brothers and sisters. I greet you in the name of my country India! As Ambassador Creses was saying, the Islamic move-ment has become a political system. I believe that they have lost the ideology of righteousness, fairness and justice for all.

In the early beginnings of Islam, the prophet Mohammed taught compassion, tolerance, and peace. The world must learn to deal with terrorism from a thought process. A good example of this is my countryman Gandhi who believed that peaceful demonstrations would eventually break down the unfair treatment from the British government. You all know the results. History has spoken, but not only has it spoken it has showed us that it works."

To everyone's surprise the speaker of the house stood up and approach the podium, whispering something in the Ambassador's ear. He stepped back from the podium.

The Other Life of Mary Abrams | 99

"I am sorry, I have to make this announcement," said the speaker of the house. "It seems that reality has joined us this afternoon. We just received a terrorist threat and we must ask all of you to evacuate the capital building immediately when this matter is cleared up, we will resume tomorrow at the same time. Thank you all for coming."

At the direction of the speaker of the house, the congregation began to break up and hurry out of the building. The Professor and the college students frantically followed the rest of the 2,000 and some visitors and guests. Finding the van, they loaded up and left the parking lot only to line up with the rest of congested traffic.

"Amazing," said Professor Hans. "The man was talking about terrorism and then we get a terrorist threat."

"Crazy," said Mary and Maggie, digging in their purses.

"Yeah," said Glenn Taste, looking out the window. "Really wild! Our very first terrorist threat."

"That's not exciting," Bill Moss said nervously shaking his leg. "It's scary!"

Pulling up in front of the hotel 20 minutes later, Larry Daniels mumbled. "It's just another day in America guys."

The group unloaded and retraced their footsteps back into the hotel.

Catching the elevator, they all went to their prospective rooms.

100 | James Edwards III

Chapter 13:

Samuel Moore

Several hours later, cell phones were ringing off the hook. Mary picking up her cell phone answered, "Hello!"

"You guys ready?" asked Daniels on the other end.

"We've been waiting on you!" said Mary. "Maggie's calling Dr. Hans to let him know we're hanging out. So, meet us at the van." Hanging up, she told Maggie to get ready.

Fifteen minutes later, the young college men were waiting at the van for the girls.

"Who's driving?" asked Glenn Taste.

"Not me," said Daniels, checking his championship watch.

"So, I gotta drive?" Bill Moss said with a *why me* look on his face.

"Looks like it's on you bro!" said Glenn and Larry grinning, as they climbed into the passenger van. Climbing into the driver's seat, Bill mumbled to himself. He started up the van, letting it idle.

"Here they come!" said Larry, winking at Maggie, as she said hello.

Mary, feeling uncertain, asked, "Are we all sure about this?"

With the usual slang, the guys said, "Let's just do it." The girls climbed into the van, buckled up and were on their way. Making their way onto the The Other Life of Mary Abrams | 101

highway, it wasn't long before they reached their exit. *Hagerstown Old Maryland*, the sign read.

"Okay Bill …" said Maggie, reading the GPS on her cell phone, "make a right here.

In a hundred yards make a left. The house should be two houses from the corner."

"Right here?" said Moss, slowing down and scratching his head.

"Right here!" said Larry. "Don't pull in front of the house."

"Look guys, let's tell her that we're doing a college survey," Mary said, looking for an excuse.

"Will that work?" said Glenn Taste. "It's 9:00."

"Well it's gonna have to work," said Maggie looking at Mary as she nodded and agreed.

Daniels, becoming agitated, said, "Let's just get it over with. Bill, you stay in the car, because she knows you."

"But it's dark out here," Moss said looking around and nervously shaking his leg.

"Tough luck," said Larry angrily, as he climbed out of the van.

"Just suck it up bro … You'll be okay." Glenn added climbing out of the van with the girls.

The college students walked down the street to 19515. Stopping and picking up something, Glenn Taste caught up with the rest of the group.

"What you find?" asked Maggie.

"Nothing …" said Glenn, smiling. "Just dirt."

Finding the house, they quietly walked up the steps and rang the door-bell. A few minutes later the door opened with an elderly woman in a floral dress with silver gray hair sitting in a wheelchair.

"May I help you?" asked the lady with concern.

"Yes ma'am," said Larry Daniels politely. "Are you Margaret Walker?"

We're here from New York State College."

102 | James Edwards III

Anxious and overly excited, Maggie blurted out. "We're here to take a survey and your name came up in our database." Larry frowned at her and shook his head.

Mary, not wanting Maggie to make the senior suspicious, began to help out. "Yes ma'am, we're sorry to disturb you this late but we attend class in the day which makes it hard to do surveys. So most of our research is done at night."

Looking a little apprehensive, the senior citizen half smiled and said

"come on in." The college students entered the house to the smell of baked meatloaf. Closing the door behind them, they waited for instructions.

"Have a seat" said the handicaped senior citizen.

"Oh, thank you! But it won't take that long," Mary said as she began introducing her classmates. "This is Larry Daniels, Glenn Taste, Maggie Werks and I am Mary Abrams."

Squinting with a telescopic stare, the old woman asked, "What did you say your name was?"

"Abrams," Mary said. "Mary Abrams."

The expression on the old woman's face read like a newspaper. She was on to them.

"Okay … kids! Is this some kind of game? You're not here for any survey, so what is it you want?"

"Just a few questions ma'am," Glenn said, shuffling over to the fireplace.

"Yes," said Maggie. "We just have a few questions."

"And what might those be?" said the old lady, with a quiver in her voice.

"Go ahead," said Larry and Maggie, looking at Mary.

"Well …" said Mary shaking. "Do you know a black man named Samuel Moore who works for Ambassador John Dorn?"

"I have no idea what you're talking about young lady, I think you all should go."

"Yes, you do," said Maggie with authority. "You were on the plane with us and someone saw you …" Her voice trailed off.

The Other Life of Mary Abrams | 103

"Saw me … saw me do what?" Hollered the silver-haired old lady.

"Hey gang!" said Larry. "Maybe we should go?"

"Look… ." said the senior citizen. "I'm just an old lady. I don't know anything."

Ignoring the pleas of Maggie and Mary for answers, she rolled herself over to the door and opened it. "I think you all better leave now!"

"Please ma'am … Do you know anything about Samuel Moore?"

begged Mary.

"I don't know any Samuel Moore."

"You're a guest of Ambassador John Dorn … just like we are," revealed Maggie.

"So what!" said the senior, rocking back and forth in her wheelchair.

Breaking the conversation, Glenn Taste got everyone's attention when he picked up a gold urn. Admiring it, he said, "This is one of the most beautiful urns I've ever seen."

"Put that down," said the wheelchair senior citizen, shaking her finger at Glenn Taste.

Glenn was positive, she knew something asked, "Nothing at all …

huh?" He removed the top of the urn.

His classmates looked in horror. Glenn reached into the urns and began dropping dirt on the hardwood floor.

"You son of a bitch," said Margaret Walker, jumping out of her wheelchair and walking over to Glenn. Snatching the urn out of his hands, Walker said, "These are my dead husbands' ashes."

The college students were bewildered that the woman could not only stand, but could *walk*. "I thought you couldn't walk!" said Maggie looking shocked as her classmates.

"I don't know anything. They told me not to talk to anyone," the elderly Margaret Walker said.

"Who told you not to talk to anyone?" asked the college students in harmony.

104 | James Edwards III

"Samuel Moore … He came to my house; that's all I can say. You better leave now."

Reaching into his pocket Glenn pulled out the rest of the dirt he had picked up outside. Showing Margaret Walker, he said "I think your husband is all there ma'am."

"Just get out," said the elderly woman, beckoning them to the door.

The college students tried to apologized for their deception and left.

Walking the short distance back to the van they began discussing Margaret Walker.

Looking at Mary and grabbing her arm, Maggie said, "Bull shit! What is she hiding?"

"Well … she did admit that there is a Samuel Moore, if that helps."

said Mary, turning to Glenn. She said, "Oh yeah, that was a slick move.

How did you know she was going to have an urn?"

"What old person doesn't have their loved one sitting around?" said Glenn laughing while Larry shook his head.

"I have to admit, nice move," said Daniels, half grinning.

Arriving at the van, Bill Moss was happy to see them. Hardly able to contain himself he asked, "So what did she say?"

"Not much," said Larry and Glenn in unison as they helped Maggie and Mary into the van.

Starting up the van, Bill pulled off into the darkness of the night.

"So, she didn't know nothing at all?" asked Bill with disappointment.

"Nada," said Larry, pointing to the stop sign. "Make a right here."

"Wait a minute … we're supposed to make a right or left back there?"

asked Mary.

"None of this looks familiar to me either," said Maggie, pulling out her cell phone to check her GPS.

Popping Bill on the back of the head. Glenn asked. "You don't remember which way we came, bro?"

The Other Life of Mary Abrams | 105

"Hey … cut it out," said Bill rubbing the back of his head, while reading street signs out loud.

"Hey guys!" said Maggie. "We're going the wrong way. Turn around, Bill"

"What?" Bill moved over to the Park Lane waited for traffic to clear and made a U-turn passing a black Cadillac SUV. 150!!!

"Whoa!" said Bill, looking in his rearview mirror. "Did you guys see that black SUV?"

"What about it?" said Maggie, putting on lipstick.

"Yeah," said Mary, checking her cell phone. "What about it?"

"Who cares!" said Larry Daniels, interrupting. "They made more than one black Cadillac SUV."

"Sure they di-d," said Bill Moss stuttering. "Well don't look now,

'cause here comes one of them."

The college students frantically turned around looking out the rearview window.

"My God!" screamed Mary. "They're following us!"

In the excitement of the students hollering directions to Bill, he turned down a dead-end street with abandoned apartment buildings on each side.

"God dammit Bill!" yelled Larry. "Now we're trapped. Hurry up turn around."

Before Bill could turn around, the black SUV drove past the street.

"Quiet!" said Glenn Taste. "I don't think they saw us."

"Whata we do now?" asked Bill, his voice quivering.

"Thank God! They didn't see us," whispered Maggie.

"Maybe we should wait a while?" said Glenn looking out the back window.

"Hell no!" said Daniels, inviting any challengers.

Gupping air before he spoke Bill said, "I agree with Glenn."

"Me too!" said Maggie and Mary.

In the dark shadows of the abandoned apartment buildings the college students didn't notice the stranger in the doorway, dressed in old jeans, 106 | James Edwards III

worn down gym shoes and a hand-me-down jacket. The vagabond stranger came out of the shadows and quietly snuck up on the van.

"Well … what do we have here?" said the vagrant pulling out a knife.

"Oh my God!" cried Maggie.

"Do something," said Mary to the guys.

Ignoring their cries for help, the man put the knife in Bill's face.

"Give me your money now," said the stranger.

"We're just college students," hollered Moss, on the verge of wetting his pants.

Suddenly, they saw headlights at the end of the street. The black Cadillac SUV had returned. The stranger was distracted by the tall dark figure getting out of the black SUV.

Suddenly, the would-be robber changed his facial expression. Staring intensely, he screamed to the top of this voice, "You see that?" The robber began shaking nervously and turning white as a ghost.

Too afraid to turn around, the college students just nodded to pacify their assailant.

"It's not my time!" Screamed the robber hysterically. "Why are you bothering me?" Dropping his knife, the thief turned and ran in between the dark buildings, ranting and raving as he disappeared in the night.

"What the hell was that?" said Larry Daniels turning around in time to see the black Cadillac SUV pull off.

"Hey guys!" Daniels said with relief in his voice. "The truck is gone!"

"Let's get the hell out of here," said the group sounding like a harmonious choir.

Bill Moss put the passenger van in reverse, with tires screeching, he backed down the street and turned around. Finding their way back to a familiar landmark, they jumped on the freeway, heading back to the hotel.

Upon arriving, they eagerly departed the van and rushed into the hotel, catching the elevator up to their floor.

The Other Life of Mary Abrams | 107

"Do you believe it?" asked Mary, emotionally drained and out of breath. "That guy could have killed us all!"

"You guys were the ones giving directions!" said Bill Moss, not wanting to take the blame. "I didn't know the street was a dead end."

Ignoring the robbery attempt Maggie shouted, "Margaret Walker must have called them; otherwise how would they have known where we were?"

"Called who?" said Daniels bending down to tie his Nike gym shoelace.

"Don't be an asshole Larry!" Maggie said, looking down at him. "Seriously Larry? The black SUV!"

Bill Moss held the open-door button as the group got off the elevator.

"Hey … we're all tired." said Larry Daniels yawning. "We'll discuss it tomorrow."

They all agreed to keep the night's events from the Professor. Exchanging the usual good nights, "See you in the morning," and "Talk to you later," they all went to their rooms.

108 | James Edwards III

Chapter 14:

The Mall

Succeeding the night's rain, the rising of the sun resembled a huge orange, with descending yellow sun rays working to heat the landscape to 55°. The Washington Finch clambered in groups, flapping their wings, fighting for position to drink from the temporary water pools that hadn't evaporated.

The morning found Professor Hans sitting in his hotel room reading a newspaper. Interrupted by his cell phone ringing and vibrating, he picked it up.

"Hello.," the Professor said, clearing his throat.

"Hello Dr. Hans? Ambassador Dorn!"

"Yes … Mr. Ambassador."

"I called to tell you that there are still some security risks and they decided to postpone today's summit meeting until tomorrow. I'm very sorry. I hope that you and your class will not be inconvenienced in any form or fashion."

"No, not at all. I'm sure that the young folks will manage the day off with no problem." said the Professor, chuckling.

"Again," said Ambassador John Dorn. "I believe I speak for the entire panel. We offer our apologies for this mishap. And I'm sure that the situation will be taken care of as soon as possible. If there are any changes for tomorrow's meeting, I will let you know."

The Other Life of Mary Abrams | 109

"Well thank you!" said Professor Hans, folding the newspaper he was reading.

"Have a good day," said Ambassador Dorn.

"You too," said the Professor, hanging up.

Having all his student's telephone numbers, he decided to call Larry Daniels.

"Hello, Mr. Daniels?"

"Yes Professor?"

"The summit meeting for today has been canceled. So … you and your classmates have the day off."

"Really!" said Daniels with excitement in his voice. "I'll let the guys know."

"Thank you, Mr. Daniels," said Professor Hans, saying goodbye.

Walking over to the table, he picked up his coffee and took a sip. *Must be serious … if they canceled the meeting.* He thought to himself. Picking up his cell phone again he dialed the ladies.

"Miss Werks?" said the Professor, hearing Maggie's voice.

"Good morning Dr. Hans," said Maggie, surprised to hear the Professor.

"Well, they've canceled the summit meeting for this morning, because of security risks. I'm sure they will work out the issues and we should resume tomorrow. In the meantime you young ladies enjoy your day off."

Maggie, ecstatic to hear the news, told the Professor thanks and hung up.

"Hey girl," said Maggie with adventure in her voice.

Lying in bed reading a book, Mary asked, "Who was that?"

Dancing around and giggling, Maggie said "Girl … we got the day off!"

"Seriously," said Mary sitting up, pushing her auburn hair out of her face.

"Yes!" screamed Maggie. "Let's hit the mall."

Jumping out of bed with excitement., the book fell on the floor. Mary began to dance with Maggie. After their brief celebration, Mary said "I don't know Mag? After last night? The robbery attempt and then the car chase, maybe we should just hang around the hotel."

110 | James Edwards III

"No way!" cried Maggie. We're gonna put that bull shit out of our minds and enjoy this day. Who showered last?"

Surrendering herself to Maggie's authoritative voice,Mary said "I think you did."

"Well then, it's your turn," said Maggie walking over to the bed, picking the book off the floor.

With teardrops hanging in her eyes Mary said. "Thanks Mag." Taking a green blouse and white khaki pants out of the closet, she hurried to the bathroom.

Looking at the book Mary was reading, Maggie was surprised it was the Bible. *Hum ...* she thought. *I guess after everything that's happened, reading this couldn't hurt.* Dismissing her present thoughts, the exhilaration of having the day off returned to her. Twenty minutes later, Mary was out of the shower.

Exiting the bathroom and wrapping her hair with a towel Mary said.

"It's all yours Mag!"

"I'll be out in a minute," said Maggie. "Oh, you better call the guys.

I'm sure they're up for it." Picking up a yellow blouse and a pair of black jeans, she headed into the bathroom.

Mary finished dressing and picked up her cell phone.

"Hello … Bill? We just got a call from Dr. Hans. No meeting today.

Maggie and I are going to the mall. We wanted to know if you guys wanta go."

"Yeah. We got the same call. Hold on a minute! Hey guys you want to go to the mall?" Mary could hear a chorus of *yeah* and *cools* in the back-ground. "Did you hear that?" Bill asked, as he put the phone back up to his ear.

"Yeah I did," said Mary. "We'll meet you guys in the lobby in an hour."

"Okay!" said Bill. "See you in hour."

The young college men's preparation of showering and getting dressed wore the hour down.

The Other Life of Mary Abrams | 111

"Where are they?" said Maggie, standing in the lobby with Mary.

Coming out of the elevator with fanfare, laughing and joking the young college men greeted the young women. Laughing and talking they continued to the van. The group seat belted in, with Larry in the drivers'

seat. He asked, "Where are we headed?"

"Chevy Chase Pavilion … according to my GPS it's 5335 Wisconsin Ave," said Maggie.

The New York State College students drove the 5.4 miles and arrived at the shopping mall. Searching and Finding a place to park, they walked the long black tarred parking lot to the door. The shopping pavilion was an encyclopedia of stores with brightly-lit window displays and multiple escalators with glass banisters and wood rails.

"Wow!" said Mary. "This is an exceptionally large mall."

"Yes! Yes! Yes!" cried Maggie. "You know what they say? The bigger the better!"

"Oh, here we go!" said Daniels, looking around the mall. "Ladies we're not staying here all day."

"Yeah. No way!" Chided in Bill Moss and Glenn Taste, taking in the huge structure.

Mary and Maggie, smiling at the guys responded, "We're off." Walking to the escalator and getting on, they rode to the second floor.

"Oh, my God … they have a *La Verne's*," said Maggie. "I really love this store!"

"Me too!" said Mary feeling some exhilaration seeing a familiar store.

Entering the store, the two walked around browsing. Mary picking up a green satin blouse, held it up to herself and asked, "What do you think Mag?"

"Oh, I like that. Who's the designer?"

"Oh Maggie. Do you really have to have all designer clothes?"

Not embarrassed, Maggie said, "Well not all my clothes. But you know as well as I do, you're going to get better quality in fashion. So! Who … is

… the … designer?"

112 | James Edwards III

Knowing she wouldn't stop until she knew, Mary gave in. Shaking her head with disappointment, Mary said, "If you must know, Larnell!"

Her eyes getting big with excitement Maggie said, "I knew it had to be a known designer. 'Cause it's such a beautiful blouse."

"Yeah okay Mag," said Mary with a sigh. "I think I'll try it on."

"I think you should," said Maggie picking up a night sky silk shawl wrap.

"I'll be back in a minute," said Mary, heading for the dressing room.

Entering the dressing room, she pulled the curtain closed. Trying on the blouse, Mary looked at herself in the mirror. Suddenly she saw the image of a young girl dressed in an off-white robe. Frightened by the image, she ran out of the dressing room.

Maggie, seeing Mary rush out of the dressing room, asked. "What's wrong? You look as if you seen a ghost."

Barely able to speak, Mary stuttered, "I saw someone in the mirror!"

Dumbfounded Maggie said, "There was someone behind you in the dressing room!"

"No!" cried Mary. "In the mirror was a blurred image of a young girl.

I couldn't see her face because she had a scarf on her head and was dressed in a grayish white robe. I think, with a brown braided belt or rope around her waist."

Frowning in concern, Maggie marched into the dressing room with Mary following. Staring in the mirror Maggie asked. "Are you sure? 'Cause I don't see anything."

Feeling embarrassed, Mary took a deep breath. "Maybe I'm just tired.

It's been a long week."

"Yes … It has," agreed Maggie. "Well the blouse looks very pretty on you. I think you should buy it."

"I guess I need some distraction," Mary said, still upset, as the two left the dressing room.

"Did you find anything?" Mary asked, feeling anxious to leave the store.

The Other Life of Mary Abrams | 113

"Yes, I did. I think I'm going to buy this shawl," said Maggie excitedly.

Tears swelling up in Mary eyes, she asked. "Mag, please don't mention the dressing room to the fellows."

Staring at her with piercing hazel eyes, Maggie assured her that she wouldn't. The two young college women headed for the cashier. Paying for the blouse and shawl they left the store. Seeing their classmates sitting near Paul's Delicatessen with packages scattered about on the floor, they headed that way.

"Hey guys!" said Maggie and Mary, happy to see their classmates.

"Hey ladies," said Glenn. "Pull up a chair and sit down."

While waiting for Mary and Maggie to sit down, Bill Moss licked a double dip chocolate ice cream cone. The girls seated at the table. Moss asked, "You girls finish shopping?"

In unison Mary and Maggie said, "I think we're done …"

Taking the top off his strawberry shake, Larry Daniels turned the cup up and finished it.

"That wasn't long," said Daniels. "What did you girls buy?"

"Just girl stuff. You wouldn't be interested, Mr. Daniels!" said Maggie.

Playing referee, Mary said. "I think I'll get a fish sandwich. Would you like one Mag?"

"Sounds good …" said Maggie. "Lots of tartar sauce. Here's ten dollars."

"I'm good," said Mary getting up from the table. "Back in a minute,"

she said walking away.

As she reached Paul's Delicatessen there were several people in line. She waited her turn, feeling uneasy. There were four people in front of her: three teenagers and a Boy Scout. Looking intensely, she recognized the boy from the award ceremony walking away from the counter with a triple dip ice cream cone. The young boy stopped and looked at her.

"May I help you little boy?" said Mary, inquisitive to his staring. The young Boy Scout continued to stare for several seconds that seemed like 114 | James Edwards III

hours not saying anything. Mary asked again, "Is there something I can help you with?" She asked, becoming nervously upset.

Smiling with an angelic face, the boy scout said, "It's good to see you again Mary."

Bewildered that the Boy Scout knew her name, she asked "Were you at the award ceremony for merit badges?" Ignoring her question, the young boy kept smiling and walked away.

Thinking to herself, Mary was baffled. *What the hell is going on. How would he know my name unless someone told him?*

"Excuse me ma'am," said the cashier. "Ma'am excuse me. Would you like to order?"

Distracted by her thoughts, she realized the cashier was talking to her.

"I'm sorry … Two fish sandwiches, one with lots of tartar sauce, a large fry and two small lemonades," said Mary, talking rapidly.

"Fries come with it darling," said the cashier.

Perplexed by the Boy Scout knowing her name, her facial expressions were like that of a mannequin.

The cashier asked, "Are you … okay?"

Coming back to reality Mary said, "Oh I'm sorry. Yes I'm okay."

"There's nothing to be sorry about darling. If you haven't done anything?"

"Yes ma'am … You're right," said Mary pulling out ten dollars.

The cook handed the cashier the wrapped fish sandwiches and fries.

The cashier bagged the sandwiches and put tops on the lemonade and set them on the counter.

"Will there be anything else, dear?" said the cashier wiping her hands on her apron.

"No, that's it," said Mary, with a faraway look in her eyes.

As the cashier gave her change, she smiled and said, "I don't know what you're going through. But it'll work out."

"Thank you," said Mary trying to smile. Paying for the food, she walked back to the table where her colleagues were.

The Other Life of Mary Abrams | 115

"Oh, you're back!" Said Glenn Taste, fixing his ponytail.

"Yes I am!" said Mary pulling out a chair and sitting down. Taking one of the fish sandwiches out of the bag, she handed it to Maggie along with a lemonade, accidentally kicking one of the fellows' bags on the floor. Mary asked. "What did you guys buy?"

With a devilish smile, Larry Daniels picked up a bag off the floor.

Opening it he showed the girls a pair of Nike gym shoes.

"Nice!" said Maggie. Checking the price tag.

"Yeah, real cool!" said Bill Moss, wanting attention. "They didn't have my size!"

"Come on Bill," said Glenn. "You're just cheap!"

"I'm not … cheap!" said Moss. "You heard the guy! They gotta order my size."

"Yeah … right!" said Daniels as he began to chuckle while the rest of the classmates smiled.

Moss turning red, slowly raised his middle finger, extending it toward Larry Daniels.

"Well I'm finished!" said Mary sounding more cheerful. "What about you Mag? Done."

"I think I'm full! Don't want to eat too much … gotta keep this figure!"

Daniels, looking her way with a flirtatious smile, said "I think you're doing a damn good job!"

Looking dreamy-eyed Maggie exhaled and said, "Thank you, Mr.

Football."

"Okay, you two!" Said Glenn. "Can we go?"

The college students all agreed that they had spent enough time at the mall and were ready to return to the hotel. Bill Moss finished up Maggie's french fries, while the rest of the group picked up their packages and personal belongings. They headed to the escalators, with Moss trailing. Down to the first floor, out the revolving exit doors to the van, seat belted in, the college students drove the 5.4 miles. Arriving at the Hay-Adams, they un-116 | James Edwards III

loaded the rental van with packages in hand and entered the hotel from the side door. Taking the service elevator up to their floor, the college students called it a day and retired to their rooms for the night.

The Other Life of Mary Abrams | 117

Chapter 16:

Ambassadors James Sandoval and Bartholomew Elebaz The following morning brought a fiery red sun that reflected in the sky, causing a red canopy that extended over most of the landscape. In the window of the Hay-Adams Hotel stood Larry Daniels taking in nature's display of art. Glenn Taste, stirring in his sleep, opened his eyes to see Daniels at the window.

"Hey man … What the hell you doing up so early?" said Taste pushing his hair back out of the face.

Fixated on the sunrise, Larry continued to stare without responding.

With his mind in dreamland, he thought about his 75 yards run against Georgia Tech. As the hero of the game, his price was a broken femur in the second half.

"Hey Larry … Hey man!" Getting up out of his cot, Glenn walked over to him.

Larry slowly turned and looked at Glenn, but acted as if he didn't see him.

"Hey man, what's up with you?"

Redirecting on Glenn, Larry said. "Nothing! everything's cool. I'll make some coffee."

Glenn, still baffled as to why it took Daniels so long to answer, said

"Yeah I could use some."

The Other Life of Mary Abrams | 119

Bill Moss subconsciously hearing the conversation between the two, began talking in his sleep: "Juice ma'am. I want juice not coffee, orange juice lady!

Getting the attention of Glenn and Larry, they looked at each other and began to chuckle. Larry, taking a fresh cup of coffee and walking over to Bill's bed, held it under his nose and whispered, "Here's your juice sir."

The aroma of the coffee infusing Moss nostrils awakened him. "What the fuck!" said Moss swinging at the cup in Larry's hand. Larry pulled the cup back, causing Moss to tumble out of bed.

"God … dammit Larry! Do you ever fucking quit?" said Moss getting up off the floor. Grabbing his pillow off the bed he threw it at Larry.

Daniels stepped out of the way and the pillow hit the coffee maker knocking it to the floor and splashing hot coffee on Larry's feet.

"You fucking asshole," said Larry angrily. Rushing toward him, he jumped over the bed grabbing Moss by the throat and began choking him.

Pulling Larry off Bill, Glenn yelled. "What the hell is wrong with you two?"

"That's what the fuck you get!" Moss said straightening up his pajamas top.

Larry stood there just seething at Bill. Suddenly there was a rapid knock on the door. Going to the door, Glenn opened it to find Professor Hans.

Startled to see the Professor so early, Glenn muffled, "Good morning Dr. Hans!"

"Good morning!" responded Dr. Hans with sternness in his voice.

"What's going on here? I heard you guys as I was coming back from the lobby to get a newspaper."

"Oh … We're all good! Just a clumsy accident." said Glenn blocking the Professor's view from Larry and Bill.

"Well I suggest that you gentlemen be more careful," said the Professor. "Since I'm here, I might as well inform you the summit meetings are back on schedule. I expect everyone to be ready by ten. Gentlemen, enjoy 120 | James Edwards III

the rest of your morning and try to live up to the title!" said the professor as he left.

The young college men exchanged remorseful glances and migrated back to their respective beds. Several hours crawled by and the men were waking up again calling out numbers for their turn to the shower. The time flew by as they dressed and caught the elevator down to the first floor for breakfast.

"Well … good morning again gentlemen," said Professor Hans seated at the table with Mary and Maggie.

"Ladies," uttered Larry Daniels.

"Morning," blurted out Glenn Taste, with his laptop in one hand and notebook in the other.

"Hey Mag. Hey Mary," said Bill Moss, barely audible.

"Good morning gen-tLe-men!" Said Maggie and Mary in harmony.

"We're going to the restroom to freshen up a bit while you guys order your breakfast. Back in a minute."

The Professor nodded as the two young collegiate students left the table. The ladies were gone for quite some time. When they returned they found an empty breakfast table. The two headed for the parking lot, where they found Professor Hans and the guys waiting for them. Getting in the van they repeated the ritual: driving the short distance past the Washington monument, past the Lincoln Memorial, past the White House creating a hypnotic trance to their destination. Before they knew it, they were exiting the van. They walked up the white marble stairs, through the hallways, past the paintings, up the stairs to their reserve seats just in time.

The speaker of the house walked to the podium. "Greetings world brothers and sisters. We the United States welcome you to the 11 Day World Summit. Would you please welcome Ambassador James Sandoval From Brazil!"

Standing 5'10 with grayish hair, dressed in an avocado green worsted wool suit, white shirt and gray tie, the Ambassador said, "Cumprimentos irm~aos e irm~as." In Portuguese meaning (greetings brothers and sisters The Other Life of Mary Abrams | 121

of the world.) There was an explosion of applause, allowing the excitement to die down. He said "I greet you in the name of Brazil. Our topic today is: the world drug crisis!"

"The world is experiencing a new age of drug addiction. For the past several years, drug abuse has grown out of control. No longer do you have to be concerned about your neighbor next door smoking pot at home; now you have to worry about him or her smoking pot while driving next to you.

Since the legalization of marijuana for medical reasons, mankind has made some breakthroughs and benefited from this plant. Marijuana has helped to treat some cancers and given extensions of pain relief to millions but we must be careful not to open a floodgate. It seems that man finds himself in a dilemma when he starts tampering with nature. Processing plants to a different metabolic state is not natural."

Suddenly the Ambassador Sandoval started to cough. The coughing continued for several seconds, causing the Ambassador to take a sip of water.

"Well!" said the Ambassador, with his handkerchief in his hand. "I guess this is a good place to stop and allow my Conrad Ambassador Bartholomew Elbaz from Sudan to finish my time, please greet him with a warm welcome." The applause slowly rising continued into a crescendo from thousands of hands.

"Greetings! World brothers and sisters. "I Asalama -alaykum!" yelled the tall thin Ambassador. Approaching the podium, he said, "I greet you in the name my country Sudan."

Dressed in a pastel yellow suit, accented with a white shirt and green pinstriped tie, he glanced down at his speech and exclaimed. "When we take a plant that the creator has given us and tamper with it we are rolling the dice. It seems that we are venturing toward opening the floodgate! We should never as proprietors of this planet allow mankind to be destroyed by man's mad scientist behavior. One of the most devastating drugs known to man is cocaine. Deriving from the cocoa plant and introduced in the 1800s., 122 | James Edwards III

they thought it was a miracle drug. My, they were wrong! The genius of man allowed him to process this plant into powder, creating the nightmare that we have today. Thank God, your President, William Taft, realized that cocaine was very addictive and talked Congress into passing the Har-rison Act which bans nonmedical use of cocaine. But laws cannot stop people from participating in dangerous experimentations of drugs. So we as human beings are obligated to one another to come up with a solution to stop the distribution of cocaine, heroin and hallucinogenic pills like Met.

These drugs are creating a community of criminals and thieves. Local jails and prisons are running over in your country and mine. I think I will stop there, I have already gone over my time. I thank you! Asalama-alaykum,"

he said to a floor-shaking applause.

" Excellent!" said Professor Hans, standing and applauding.

Glenn Taste, sitting next to Maggie, leaned over and said, "One more to go …"

"One more what?" said Maggie, as she stood up to join a standing ovation.

"One more summit meeting," said Glenn standing as the crowd continued cheering and clapping.

Professor Hans, looking down the aisle at his students, motioned for them to follow him.

Exiting the auditorium, the Professor and the students fought their way through the mobs of people. Looking back, the Professor saw the class getting split up from all the people pushing and shoving.

"Grab each other's hands," said Professor Hans. Taking the Professor's advice, they managed to regroup and make it out of the building to the parking lot. Locating the van, they all climbed in and headed back to the Hey-Adams. Arriving 40 minutes later, they exited the van and entered the hotel. Catching the elevator to their floor, they joked with the Professor as they headed to their hotel rooms.

"See you in the morning, Professor," hollered the college students.

The females and males separated and went to their own rooms.

The Other Life of Mary Abrams | 123

Upon entering their hotel room Maggie walked over to the counter and picked up a bag of chips. While Mary walked over to the sofa and sat down putting her feet up on the coffee table she said, "So! One more day!"

"Yeah … That's what Glenn was saying," said Maggie, as she tore open the bag of chips. "We should celebrate tonight!"

"Yeah we should," said Mary. "Just one more day … I'll be so glad to get back home."

"Me too," said Maggie. "Hey … how about we go out tonight?"

"Where?" said Mary.

" I heard they got this way-out nightclub here in DC called … how about this: the 910 club!"

"The what?" said Mary, paying more attention.

"The 910 club," said Maggie, picking up her phone. "I heard it's the coolest club in DC."

"Yeah I bet. Where did you hear that from?" asked Mary.

"No, really one of the guys I met that works here told me about it."

"A guy you met. That works here?" said Mary with suspicion.

"Yes Mary, a guy I met here."

"Oh Mag, you're always meeting someone!"

"Well whatever. I'll call and make reservations."

"And what about the guys?" Mary said, biting her nails.

"We'll call 'em later and drag them along," said Maggie.

Maggie proceeded to dial the number and make reservations for 9:00

p.m. that evening.

As the day slipped into night the girls began to get ready to go out.

"Maggie! Did you call the guys?" asked Mary.

"Yeah. They're gonna meet us in the lobby. Hurry up and get dressed."

Checking their attire in the mirror, the two ladies finished putting on their makeup and made their way out the door.

124 | James Edwards III

Chapter 15:

The Night Club

The DC night brought in a light and sound exhibit with lightning flashes and rumbling thunder. The results of the weather caused some power failure throughout the city. Thick fog coming in from the East Coast joined up with the static electricity filling the air. The moon took the night off.

Yet the darkened streets with Friday night traffic didn't hinder the college rented van from reaching its destination at 815 V Street, located in the old warehouse district. Finding an unpaved parking lot filled with mud holes and gravel, the college students managed to squeeze in a parking space.

Departing the van, they walked the short distance to the 910 Club, as they came to what appeared to be an old factory building with over hanging spotlights half lit. Seeing a long line of people was a telltale sign where the entrance was. Finding themselves standing in line with over a hundred people, their faces reflected their disappointment.

"My God!" said Maggie, "We'll never get in!"

"All I know is they better have food!" Bill Moss said, squawking.

"Shut up bro!" mumbled Glenn Taste, smiling at a female stranger in line.

"We'll get in!" Daniels said with confidence, turning his collar up.

"Sure we will," said Mary. "You guys gotta have faith!"

The Other Life of Mary Abrams | 125

At that moment, a 6'5 Arnold Schwarzenegger look-alike dressed in a dark black suit approached the crowd asking for Mary Abrams.

"I'm Mary Abrams," Mary said looking startled. "Who are you?"

"Never mind who I am!" responded the 6'5 stranger with authority.

"I've been sent to escort you into the club!"

"Well who sent you?" demanded Mary.

"Ambassador Dorn! Now would you please follow me?" growled the look-alike.

Looking puzzled, Mary and her classmates obeyed the muscle build stranger.

Walking pass the crowds of people, you could hear mumbling of pa-trons. Some of them in line for hours, made faces at the group of college students going before them. Following the tall stranger inside, the students trailed him down a dark hallway with fluorescent green lights along the floor that led to the main room. As they drew closer they could hear music blaring: "Love is not weak; awake from your sleep. We have to seek higher ground. What kind of mother would not love but rather, watch her son dying in the street. Left is her daughter, but she's out of order, no one took the time to teach." Welcoming them to the party and reaching the ballroom with red yellow and green strobe lights flashing, Arnold Schwarzenegger's look-alike pushed past the movers and shakers on the dance floor. He lead the college students to a candlelit table in the center of the room, receiving thanks from the students. The escort retreated, leaving them in an atmosphere of excitement and adventure.

"I can't believe it," exclaimed Maggie, pulling out her chair. "We got in!"

"I told you, we would!" said Mary, taking a seat and picking up a menu.

"Okay … So we're in," said Moss, refusing to sit down. "Where's the food?"

"Dammit Moss! What the fuck is wrong with you?" said Larry Daniels, sitting down. "Is that all you think about?"

"Nooo!" said Moss turning red-faced, thinking about his father screaming and yelling at him for eating so much at the family restaurant.

126 | James Edwards III

Not wanting the two to get into another argument, Glenn Taste interrupted.

"Hey Moss! If you need an escort, I'll go with you." Glenn said smiling sincerely.

"I don't need a fucking escort!" Moss said, seething.

"Calm down, bro!" said Glenn getting up from his seat. "I'm just bull-shitting with you!"

Angry and feeling embarrassed, Moss managed to say. "Sorry."

"We'll be back," said Glenn. "You guys want anything?"

"We're good right now," said their classmates in harmony. "Yeah guys go ahead. Find something to eat. We'll order drinks!" said Mary, putting the menu down.

As the two left on their venture to find food, Maggie leaned over and yelled to Mary "Maybe Mossy does have a food problem?"

Responding, Mary said, "I can hardly hear you. The music is so loud!"

"For-get it!," hollered Maggie.

Leaning in closer Mary asked, "What did you?"

"Never mind. It's not that important," said Maggie turning to Larry Daniels and yelling. "Are you a celebrity sports player or a college student tonight? Cause we need a waiter."

Not appreciating Maggie's sarcasm, Larry felt the need to ignore her question. "Do I have a choice?" Daniels said, pushing his chair back and standing up, raising his voice to compete with the music. He said, "I assume you ladies want the usual."

"Wine for me," said Mary. "Cabernet."

"The same for me, handsome!" said Maggie flirtatiously.

Taking the instructions with a smile, Daniels leaned down and whispered into Maggie's ear and left.

Squinting and shaking her head, Mary said, "You two!"

Smiling and blushing, Maggie changed the subject. "Oh by the way! I love your outfit. Is that Christian Dior?"

The Other Life of Mary Abrams | 127

"Yes, darling I gave in," said a smiling Mary. Dressed in a satin pink form-fitting dress that blossomed out right above the knees, Mary's long slender legs were accented with dust-gray shoes and matching purse. They rose her to model status.

"'Bout time," said Maggie. " You know girl, you gotta look the part."

Smiling and laughing Mary said, "Thank you."

"Well," said Maggie, positioning herself. "This is Ralph Lauren! I bought it on sale at this little shop." Standing up, she said, "Check it out

… orange blouse, tan suede pants … orange and gray necklace that accents my Celine Paris purse, and you know I wouldn't be caught in anything but Christian Louboutn stilettos."

Admiring Maggie's outfit. Mary said with some humor in her voice,

"Very nice! Mag, Very nice!"

"Thank you, Mary," said Maggie, blushing as she sat down.

"So, who's here tonight?" asked Mary.

"I believe Edward J; you know he's in town! We saw him in the lobby,"

hollered Maggie above the music.

Their conversation was cut short by a bubbly red headed waitress.

"Excuse me ladies, but this handsome gentleman in VIP sent these drinks over to you."

"Real-ly!" said Maggie. "And who might that be?"

"Ambassador Dorn!" said the waitress, sitting the champagne on the table.

"He's here!" cried Mary, hysterically.

"Yes he is," said the waitress, placing the last glass of champagne on the table and taking out pad and pencil. Writing something down, she smiled at the two and departed.

"You know what Maggie? I think I need to thank Mr. Dorn in person."

"Well wait a minute. Wait till the guys get back," Maggie said, anticipating a showdown.

"For what!" said Mary. "I'm a big girl. I can handle myself. Besides I have a lot of questions for Ambassador Dorn. Picking up one of the champagne
128 | James Edwards III

glasses Mary turned it up. Slamming the glass down, she stood up and adjusted her clothing and hair. Ignoring Maggie's pleas, she left in pursuit of Ambassador Dorn.

Minutes later, pushing through the crowd and making his way to the table, Daniels with a tray of drinks in hand asked, "So where is Mary?"

Trying to get her words out and stuttering Maggie's exclaimed, "She just ran off!"

Looking confused Larry asked, "What do you mean she ran off?"

"I mean, she went to talk to Ambassador Dorn."

"What the hell for? The guys a fucking dignitary, she'll never get to see him."

"Dorn sent drinks to our table," Maggie blubbered.

"So what! Who gives a fuck! It's free ain't it."

"Larry please," Maggie said, feeling the need to rescue her friend.

Picking up a glass of champagne and downing it, Larry blurted out,

"Who cares. She can handle herself. Let her go over there and blow off some steam. If by some miracle she does get to see him, maybe she can find out what the hell's been going on since we left New York."

" Well! Say what you want. But we do know that Samuel Moore works for Dorn and Moore told Margaret Walker not to say anything. Dorn has to be involved in this or have some knowledge of what's going on. So …

what she's doing could be very dangerous."

"You mean fraternizing with the enemy? That's strange," Larry said calming down and smiling. "'Cause if you look over your shoulder, you'll see Mary and some guy dancing on the dance floor."

"Where?" asked Maggie, getting excited and turning around. "My God … She's dancing with Dorn!"

"So, that's Ambassador Dorn?"

"Yes, it is..." Maggie said looking dreamy-eyed. "Oh yeah! That's right.

You never met Dorn."

The Other Life of Mary Abrams | 129

Having an ego, steroids moment, Larry said, "Looks as though I didn't miss anything!"

"Yeah … You would say that. I think he's so handsome."

"Yes. I can see how she could be in danger!" Larry said sarcastically.

"Why don't we just give them some competition?" Grabbing Maggie by the hand, he pulled her out on the dance floor.

The two tried to dance their way over to Mary and Ambassador Dorn, but the crowd was too boisterous and only allowed them to get within yelling distance.

"Hey Mary!" yelled Maggie, as she caught a glimpse of her.

Mary, seeing Maggie, cupped her hands and hollered something back, but Maggie couldn't hear her. Watching Mary and the Ambassador dancing and laughing she felt relieved for the moment.

"Hey!" said Ambassador Dorn. "Let's get off this dance floor and find somewhere where we can talk." Mary agreed. They left the dance floor and found a quiet spot near the stairs leading to the rooftop atrium.

"Okay Ms. Abrams … You said you have some questions for me."

"Well," said Mary feeling nervous, "I apologize for being so rude and interrupting your private party, and I thank you for getting us in the club, but some strange events have taken place since we left New York and I'm just trying to find some answers."

In the meantime, Glenn Taste and Bill Moss full of chicken tenders and french fries returned to an empty dining table.

Puzzled and looking around for familiar faces, Glenn asked "Where the hell is everybody at?"

"Don't ask me," moaned Moss, picking up two glasses of champagne and turning them up.

"Well bro, we don't need no more twilight zone shit!" Glenn announced, watching Bill pick up another glass of champagne and turning it up.

Knowing Moss not to be a big drinker Glenn said, "Hey bro, slow down!"

130 | James Edwards III

"Slow down for what? I'm just having a little fun cheer," said Moss picking up a fourth glass and drinking that down.

"Whoa, man I really feel that," said Moss slurring his speech."Awe …

shit! I think I'm going to be sick."

"Dammit Moss," said Glenn, watching his classmate turned green.

"Hey bro, I think it stopped raining. Let's go on the rooftop and get some air."

Glenn took Bill by the arm to stabilize him. They pushed their way through the crowds of people on the dance floor and made it to the stair-well leading upstairs to the rooftop atrium, passing Mary and Ambassador Dorn. Seeing the two, Moss yelled, "Hey … Ma-ry, looking good!" Going up the stairs, Glenn kept Moss from falling by getting behind him as they took step-by-step to the abandoned rooftop. Sitting Moss at a table with a canopy and chairs close to the protective security wall, Glenn took in the night's silhouette of the city. Bill Moss, face down on the table, began mumbling something.

"What you say, bro?" asked Glenn, tightening up his ponytail with another rubber band.

"I said … nobody likes me … cause I'm fat."

"Hey man, that's not true!"

Sitting up and holding his face in his hands, Bill asked, "Who then?"

Feeling as if he's been put on the spot Glenn spoke out. "I don't know, bro. I like you."

Moss began speaking through the alcohol he had consumed.

"Noooo. Nobody likes me! Larry picks on me because I'm fat and I don't play sports!"

"Hey bro! Who gives a fuck about Larry? He's a privileged, conceited, sports-playing asshole."

Not knowing the longtime relationship between the two, Glenn had no idea that Moss had been trying to get Larry's approval from the time that they met. Jumping up from the table, Moss kicked the chair backwards The Other Life of Mary Abrams | 131

making it fall over. He then walked over to the safety wall and climbed up on the top of it.

"Bro! Have you lost your mind? Get the fuck down!" a nervous Glenn Taste said.

"Naw … I haven't lost it. It's right here with me!" said Bill Moss, laughing as he walked on top of the safety wall.

"Get down bro! Before you get hurt," Glenn said, getting scared. Realizing the seriousness of the situation he sent a 911 text that read, "Come to the rooftop, emergency," to his college classmates.

With the loud music and Mary's phone being in her purse on vibrate, she didn't get the text. Engulfed in conversation with Ambassador Dorn she asked, "Do you know a lady named Margaret Walker?"

"I don't believe I do," said the Ambassador.

"Well," she said, "your aid Samuel Moore made a visit to her house."

Mary looked for signs of involvement on the Ambassador's face.

"Really," replied Ambassador John Dorn. "Well … let me ask you, does this Margaret Walker have any political ties to any organizations?"

Feeling suspicious, Mary responded, "I don't know her personally. So, I wouldn't know who or whom she's affiliated with."

Moving closer, the Ambassador took Mary's hands and held them.

Looking deep into her eyes. He said "I assure you, you have nothing to worry about. There are some mysteries in life that we are unaware of and sometimes strange things happen but you are in no danger."

Swooning under the hypnotic stare and baritone bass coming out of this handsome face, Mary surrendered her curiosity as the Ambassador moved within inches of her lips. Abruptly stopping, Ambassador Dorn said,

"Your phone is vibrating."

Disappointed, Mary exclaimed, "My phone! My phone's in my purse on vibrate! You can hear that?"

Ignoring her question the Ambassador said, "I think you need to answer that!"

132 | James Edwards III

Mary opened her purse and took her phone out. Reading the text she said, "I'm sorry but I have to go. I just got an emergency message from one of my classmates to come to the rooftop."

"I hope it's nothing too serious," said Ambassador Dorn. He looked for the stairs leading to the rooftop. Seeing the sign rooftop atrium he said,

"Come on. I'll go with you."

The two rushed up the stairs. Arriving on the rooftop, they saw a scene that looked like something out of a movie.

"Look at me … See, I got skills," Moss said, intoxicated as he walked on top of the security wall two stories up.

Shaking nervously as she approached the two, Mary exclaimed, "Bill Moss you get down from there right now!"

Surprised to see Mary, Bill became distracted as he looked her way.

Stumbling and slipping off the top of the wall, he managed to grab hold of the ledge before he fell over to the street below.

Glenn Taste, being the closest to Bill, rushed over and grabbed one of his hands as he hung on to the wall two stories up.

"God dam-mit, bro," hollered Glenn, as he tried to pull Moss back up.

Bill being hysterical, cried out. "Somebody help me!"

"I'm trying," said Glenn struggling to hold Moss. Losing his grip Glenn yelled. "I can't hold him, somebody help me!"

Maggie reaching the rooftop with Larry in tow, yelling, "What the hell is going on?"

Ignoring her, everyone stayed focused on the situation.

Ambassador Dorn rushed over to the wall to help Glenn.

"He's slipping," cried Glenn, as he slipped out of his hands.

Pushing Glenn out of the way, Ambassador Dorn reached over the wall and pulled Moss back to safety. Surrounded by all of his classmate except Larry, Moss was still in an alcohol stupor. Breathing a sigh of relief.

He thanked and hugged Ambassador Dorn, getting sympathy from his classmates except Larry. He wondered where he was.

The Other Life of Mary Abrams | 133

Slurring his speech, he asked, "Where's Mr. Football?"

Maggie, surprised at Bill's question turned around looking for him. "I don't know," said Maggie. "He was right behind me coming up the steps."

Somewhat puzzled as to where Larry could be, the students refocused and helped their classmate down the steps back to the main ballroom. They struggled to get Bill back to their table. They sat him down and gave him some coffee.

"Well," said Ambassador Dorn to the college students, "I'm glad everything turned out okay."

Turning to Mary and smiling he said, "Here's my number. Call me tomorrow after the summit meeting and we'll continue our conversation."

Mary, taking the Ambassador's business card, said she would call. The students continued thanking Ambassador Dorn who smiled and accepted their praise. He left and headed back to the VIP section. From out of nowhere, Daniels showed up.

"Where the hell you been, Larry?" asked Mary and Maggie.

"I went to get help," said Larry, feeling the anger from his classmates.

"Where's the help, bro," said Glenn raising his voice.

Squinting and giving Glenn a threatening stare, Larry grumbled, "Like I said … I went to get help!"

"Hey …" said Bill Moss, "I think I'm gonna to be sick!"

"Don't you dare," said Maggie, fanning Bill. "You've already ruined the night."

"Well gang, I think we should call it a night," said Mary feeling sorry for Moss.

"I agree," said Glenn. "Although, tomorrow is the last day of the summit. We still got the weekend."

"Yeah," stated Larry getting up from the table. "Yes, we do, don't we?

Got the weekend left. Sure in the hell don't wanta lose anyone now, do we?"

Larry's classmates, not knowing how to take his comments, gathered their things and decided to leave. Helping Bill to his feet, Maggie and Mary 134 | James Edwards III

took each arm as Glenn cleared the crowd to get him to the exit. Making their way down the street to the parking lot, the three of them helped Moss into the van while Larry got behind the wheel and chauffeured them back to the hotel.

The Other Life of Mary Abrams | 135

Chapter 16:

The Last Summit Meeting

With the sun's assignment to rise in the east, it went beyond its duty, bringing the early morning to a pleasant 65°, erasing the inclement weather from the night before. Cosigning the improvement of the weather was the Washington Goldfinch in tree branches serenading early morning joggers.

The bright solar planet slowly rose, aiming its rays at the Hey-Adams Hotel where sounds of moaning could be heard coming from Room 304.

"Aw man! I feel like shit!" said Bill Moss. "Hey guys," hollered Moss., getting up off the side of the bed. Opening the bedroom door, Moss staggered down the hallway to the living room.

"Hey Glenn … hey Larry!" hollered Moss looking around. *Where the hell is everybody at?* He thought to himself. Walking over to the sink, he poured a glass of water and drank it. Looking on the counter he saw a note saying, "We're at breakfast."

Breakfast! Bill thought. *Aww … fuck, I'm gonna throw up.* Rushing to the bathroom Moss threw up in the toilet. Getting up off his knees, he washed his face in the sink and sat on the toilet seat for a few minutes.

Feeling somewhat better, he took a shower and got dressed. Checking around the room to see if he had left anything, Moss grabbed his book bag and headed out the door. Catching the elevator down to the first floor he

headed to the dining room. Greeted by smiles and snickering, Moss pulled out a chair and sat quietly.

"Well young man … I'm glad to see you could make it," said the Professor with a smile. "Your classmates tell me you had quite a night?"

"Yes sir … I know I over did it," said Bill covering his face with his hands.

"Well … I'm glad you had a good time, but there are times when a man, or woman for that matter, should curtail their drinking," said the Professor, taking a sip of coffee.

"I think, I've learned my lesson," Bill said uncovering his face. "I know it was foolish of me to climb."

Cutting off Bill's sentence Maggie injected, "Clown around, yeah Bill!

You shouldn't have drunk so much and been clowning around." Catching on to Maggie's divergence of him climbing on top of the security wall, he played along with her.

"Right, right, you're right Maggie."

"I won't be getting drunk and no more clowning around," Moss said, wiping sweat from his forehead. "I have truly learned my lesson."

"Wise decision young man," said the Professor. "I'm sure your classmates agree. Would you like to order breakfast?"

Almost turning green, Bill shook his head and said. "No thank you, sir."

"Well class, since this is the last summit meeting, I would like to thank you all for conducting yourselves as adults and displaying your manners.

Our flight doesn't leave until Sunday night. You will have all day Saturday and early Sunday morning to enjoy yourselves. I know you're all anxious to get back home and so am I. Now without any further ado, shall we go?"

Rising from the table, the students gathered their belongings and followed the Professor through the lobby out to the parking lot. Locating the Rental, they climbed in. As usual, Larry drove. Reaching the capital building, they pulled in the parking lot and unloaded. Locking the van, Mary, Maggie and Larry joked and teased one another while Glenn and Bill Moss 138 | James Edwards III

remained quiet. They followed the Professor up the marble steps into the building, through the crowded lobby, up to the balcony. Not seeing their familiar usher, they managed to get to their seats. The anxiety of going home motivated the students into constant chatter.

"Last one," said Maggie putting on lip gloss.

"Thank God," said Mary taking her phone out and putting it on vibrate.

Turning to Bill, Glenn, and Larry sitting down the row from her, Mary asked "Why so quiet guys? Aren't you homesick?"

Larry responded with a smile and said, "Home is where the heart is."

Getting no response from Glenn and Bill, she turned her attention to the podium.

"Greetings world brothers and sisters. We the United States would like to welcome you to the last day of the 11 Day World Summit."

"Hey," said Maggie. "What happened to the speaker of the house?

How come Ambassador Dorn is opening the summit?"

"I don't know," said Mary, getting excited and running her fingers through her hair.

Professor Hans looked down the aisle and shushed them.

"I would like to introduce you to one of the most influential humani-tarians that I have ever met, my friend and yours. Please give a warm welcome to our last speaker of the summit, Ambassador Peter Cresas."

Standing 6 feet tall, dressed in a dark gray suit with purple tie and white shirt, the Ambassador said "thank you" in Hebrew.

"Welcome world brother and sisters! I greet you in the name of my country Israel!"

You could feel the electricity in the air as people began standing and clapping for the last speaker. "There are mysteries in life that we are unaware of and sometimes strange things happen. As a world society, we must be prepared for the unseen," said Ambassador Cresas.

Mary, hearing familiar, words began thinking of the conversation she had with Ambassador Dorn the night before.

The Other Life of Mary Abrams | 139

"I will be giving a summation of the topics we've had for the past ten days, and adding one," said the Ambassador, flipping through the pages of his notes. He said, "I would like to speak to you today about the rebirth of man. As a world society, we must change our way of thinking. Take for instance our food crisis. This planet has enough land to grow food for all the inhabitants of Earth. Yet we have a crisis, a shortage. Why? Because man's appetite for more has gotten out of control. Forgive me, I don't want to offend anyone but the excessive eating must be contained. The average person on this planet is 30 pounds overweight. This is the results of a lack of discipline. Scientists have told us, the less calories a person consumes the longer they will live. Why? Because it allows the body to rest and not be overworked by having to store food it doesn't need. Yes, man is in this predicament because of his greed, which can only be overcome by changing his way of thinking. It's all in the mindset my brothers and sisters. It's all about how we perceive life, of course some things are a necessary evil.

Like man's inventions for transportation, along with other inventions of manufacturing. The results! We are suffocating on our own planet. We have creative alternatives to the energy source that we are now using. It is estimated at this point, if we continue using our resources at the present rate, we will run out; man must change his ways of thinking. As human beings, we have separated ourselves from one another and demanded individuality. But this is not good for the whole of mankind when it comes to transportation. Now the situation is becoming dire. We must consider less manufacturing of individual transportation and focus on mass transit.

Don't miss understand me. I am aware that we will lose some manufacturing jobs but we must not be afraid of the challenge. I believe wholeheart-edly that man's ingenuity will sustain him in his endeavor. As custodians of this planet we must do our best to take care of it. If we don't, where will we live? It's all about working together as a civilization. Unity is a must if we are to survive. We must work with other nations for the whole of the planet. Let us put away our differences and stop the bickering, which leads 140 | James Edwards III

to a violent society. The anger and unlawful acts against one another cannot continue.

"Is there any doubt, that crime has systemic roots in economics; that lack of education gives birth to unemployment, which ushers in civil un-rest? With crime running rampant, it forces society to build prisons that are filled with desperate people who were trying to earn a living unlawfully. The money that is spent on building these warehouses to house people could be given to educate the masses. But big business is determined to do anything in its power to generate profits, even if that means overloading society with enormous debt. Should we have a lower cap on interest rates and a set amount of profits that these large corporations can generate? Think about it … Do we have any other options? We must change our way of thinking. It's not about us as individuals, but it's about surviving on a dying planet. One of the oldest books known to man tells us that if we want to see changes then we must change and not be the people we were but a new people with vision. The governments of this planet have not been great stewards; otherwise we would not be in this predicament. If our governments cannot serve us, we have an obligation to one another to have them removed, either by submission or by force.

Haven't we learned from our history? Our past? Or shall we continue drowning in our over indulgence of material substance? It is written 'man does not live by bread alone.' We have an obligation to future generations, for if we leave a prosperous legacy, we are only preparing a place for future generations to thrive and continue mankind's elevation. Man's creativity is generated by his inner being, his spirit. So therefore, the spiritual man must be nurtured for growth," said Ambassador Cresas with thunderous applause following.

Ambassador John Dorn stood up and slowly walked to the platform, whispering something into the ear of Ambassador Cresas. As the applause died down Ambassador Cresas said, " I thank you for your attendance and your undivided attention during these summit meetings. May the Lord The Other Life of Mary Abrams | 141

God Jehovah bless you all and see you returned safely back to your nations and families."

The people stood up and gave a ten-minute standing ovation, clapping, whistling, and cheering.

"Well," said Professor Hans clapping along with the mass of people.

Turning to his students he hollered, "Very educational. I believe we have all learned something. At least, I hope we have!" As the applause died down, people began leaving. Professor Hans motioned for the students to follow him. Seeing and pushing through the crowds of some old familiar faces for the last ten days, the college students and the Professor made it out of the building, down the marble stairs out to the parking lot to the van. Climbing in the van they all buckled in and drove through the DC

streets of great monuments back to the Hey-Adams hotel. The group departed the van and entered the hotel. Catching the elevator to their floor and exiting, they stood in the hallway.

Smiling the Professor said, "Well, I hope these summit meetings have given you some insights to the workings of our society and will help you reach your personal goals. Well … any plans for tonight?"

"No plans," said Larry, speaking up. "At least not for me."

Larry's classmates agreed with him by nodding and facial expressions.

"Yeah we're all tired," said Mary. "We'll just hang out at the hotel."

"Tonight," said Maggie with a mischievous smile. "But we got the weekend!"

"Okay," said the Professor smiling, "You young folks have a good night. I'm going to retreat to my room."

As the Professor turned and walked down the hall, the students refocused on one another. "Who's room? Guys or gals?" said Maggie, taking out her key card.

"Guys!" said Larry Daniels .

"Cool," said Mary. "We'll be down." Several hours later the young coeds were knocking on the door of 304. Larry Daniels opened the door.

142 | James Edwards III

"Hey ladies. Come on in," Moss, sitting on the floor typing on his computer, looked up to acknowledge his classmates with a smile. But Glenn remained silent with no facial expression, sitting in a chair looking out the window.

Maggie and Mary walked over to one of two flowered sofas and sat down on it. Putting their feet up on the coffee table, Maggie asked, "You guys got any popcorn?" Waiting for a response, Bill Moss got up off the floor and reached into his book bag, pulling out four bags of popcorn. Moss threw the popcorn across the room to Maggie. She caught one of the bags, not caring about the others falling to the floor. She got up and walked to the microwave.

"Man," said Larry "I can't wait to get home!"

"Me too," said Mary, with relief in her voice.

"Me three," said Bill Moss, cheering up and smiling. "What about you Glenn?"

Looking out the window, Glenn was transfixed, hearing Moss's question but not answering.

"What's up with him?" said Larry, as he walked over to the other sofa across from Maggie and Mary and plopped down.

"Who knows?" said Maggie. At that moment, the hotel phone rang.

Bill Moss got up off the floor and walked over to the phone and picked it up. "Hello?" Pausing he said, "Just a moment. It's for you, Mary!"

With an inquisitive look Mary asked "Who is it?"

"I don't know," said Moss. "They asked for you."

Wondering who could it be, Mary walked over to Bill and took the phone.

"Hello?"

"Hello! Miss Abrams, this is John Dorn. How are you?"

"I'm fine," said Mary, making happy face expressions.

"I have some free time for the next several days and was wondering if you would like to join me for dinner."

The Other Life of Mary Abrams | 143

"I would love to," said Mary excitedly. "When?"

"Perhaps this evening, if you have no plans?"

"Yes... I'm free this evening."

"Great!" said Ambassador Dorn. "I'll send a limo to pick you up."

Hanging up, Mary rushed over to the sofa and picked her purse up.

She announced,

"Hey guys, I just got invited to dinner by Ambassador Dorn and it looks like I'll be seeing you all later, don't wait up for me!"

"What? You can't be serious Mary, " said Maggie standing up.

"Serious as a heart attack," said Mary laughing. "I'll see you guys later," rushing out the door she didn't give her classmates a chance to comment.

"She must be crazy as hell," said Larry Daniels, staring at Maggie.

"She's got to be!" said Bill Moss chiming in. "With all the shit that's been going on, why the hell would she go out with him?"

Suddenly, as if coming out of a trance, Glenn Taste said, "Fraternizing with the enemy could have some benefits."

"Well," said Maggie. "Welcome back. We thought you were ignoring us."

"No … Not ignoring you, just thinking."

"About what?" said Daniels, standing up and picking a bag of popcorn off the floor as he walked over to the microwave.

"I'm confused about last night," Glenn said, putting his hands behind his head.

"What's so confusing about me getting drunk and almost killing myself? You saved my life!" said Moss.

Turning the swivel chair from the window Glenn said, "I couldn't hold you!"

"Huh … what do you mean?" Said Maggie, getting more interested.

"What I mean," said Glenn getting upset, "is Bill slipped out of my hands."

"You're crazy too! How the hell could Mossy slip out your hands and not fall to the ground?" stated Daniels.

"You're exactly right, bro … That's the question."

144 | James Edwards III

"Are you telling us that Bill slipped out of your hands."

"Exactly," said Glenn Taste.

"Okay then. Why didn't he fall?" said Daniels, checking the microwave.

"That's the confusing part. He stayed suspended in air until Dorn reached over and pulled him up."

"You're fucking crazy," said Larry Daniels chuckling. "It's your imagination you were drinking to."

"No! Hold on Larry," said Maggie. "Maybe not."

Interrupting the debate, Bill Moss said. "I hardly remember anything."

"Well … it happened," said Glenn Taste.

"Impossible," said Larry, taking popcorn out of the microwave and walking back over to the sofa and sitting down.

"Impossible or not," said Maggie, "Somehow we're gonna get to the bottom of this. Let's just hope Mary knows what she's doing. This *eye spy* shit has to stop. No one should be following anyone. Maybe, just maybe, Dorn has the answers. As the conversation wore on between the four, Glenn in the chair and Moss lying on the floor, both had nodded off to sleep.

"Okay, Maggie!" said Larry yawning. "I think we should call it a night."

"Yeah I agree," said Maggie, getting up from the sofa. You wanta walk me to my room?"

"Sure," said Larry, grabbing his key card, turning the light out, leaving his roomies in the dark. As he escorted Maggie down the hallway, there was no verbal exchange. Walking slowly to extend the time with one another, they reached Room 301. Maggie swiped her key card opening the door. Turning to Larry she said, "Good."

Her words were cut in half by Daniels' forceful lips upon hers. Shocked by his abruptness, but wanting it all the same, Maggie's reservations slowly dissolved. The two bodies intertwined, finding their way through the threshold, kicking the door closed. They paused for a moment, looking into one another's eyes for equal assurance. They tore off their clothes as The Other Life of Mary Abrams | 145

they rushed to the bed. Falling into it, they began tongue kissing with the feverish passion of uncontrollable hormones. Feeling Maggie's breasts pulsating with blood rushing into her nipples, Larry filled her with himself.

Moans of release and the slowing of rapid heartbeats signaled the sexual climactic episode was over.

146 | James Edwards III

Chapter 17:

The Discernment

With dark gray clouds and some chilling winds that hung around from the night before, there was no morning sun. The day was dark. The morning sunrays had given up trying to reach the Hey-Adams Hotel, but the winds had no trouble taking its place, as they forcefully brushed up against the hotel window of Professor Luas Hans, stirring him out of his sleep as he screamed, "Who art thou Lord?" Realizing he was dreaming, he thought to himself, *how much more of this can I take before going insane*? Getting out of bed, he picked up his cell phone. He walked into the bathroom. Sitting the cell phone on the counter, he unbuttoned his pajama bottoms and relieved himself. After washing his hands, he picked up his cell phone and called Larry Daniels.

"Hello?"

"Mr. Daniels? Professor Hans! I would like to meet with all of you this morning. It's urgent, I want all of you in my hotel room in an hour! Do you understand?"

"Yes sir! I'll tell everyone we'll be there in an hour," said Larry, wondering what the hell was so important, hanging up.

The Professor laid his phone on the counter, picking up a bar of soap.

He washed and rinsed his face. Taking a dry towel, he began patting it dry.

The Other Life of Mary Abrams | 147

After removing the towel, he looked in the mirror. Startled at the image he seen he cried, "Lord help me."

Turning off his cell phone seconds after talking to the Professor, Larry was still puzzled by the Professor's instructions. Before he could wake up Bill and Glenn, there came a pounding on the door. Rushing to the door in his underwear, he wondered who could be banging at this hour. Larry opened the door; to his surprise stood Maggie. She pushed him out of the way and rushed through the door. Standing in the middle of the living room where Bill and Glenn were still asleep from the night before. She cried, "Mary didn't come in last night! I tried calling her and I keep getting her voicemail."

Moss and Glenn, waking up from there nightly positions, sat up.

"What?" said Larry closing the door and walking over to the arm of the sofa sitting on it.

"She didn't come in last night!"

"Where could she be?" said Maggie hysterical.

"Look Mag," said Glenn Taste, trying to distract her anxiety. She's a grown woman and besides she was with Ambassador Dorn. What could possibly go wrong?" agreeing with Glenn, Bill Moss simply nodded.

"I don't think Mary staying out all night is the problem," Larry said.

"I just got a call from Dr. Hans telling me that he wants all of us in his room in the next hour and that's mandatory."

"Really bro?" said Glenn as he got up off the sofa and walked over to the refrigerator taking, out a carton of orange juice and pouring a glass.

Turning the glass up and drinking it all down at once he responded, "Aaaaw shit, bro! That's good! You know it's too close to going home for urgencies; what could be so important?"

"Well … the hell with the urgency! I'm concerned about Mary, and where the hell she is!" said Maggie, walking to the sofa and sitting down.

"I'm tired," said Bill Moss. "I just wanta go home. I'm tired of this mystery shit."

148 | James Edwards III

Ignoring Moss's whining, Larry picked up the remote off the coffee table and turned on the flat-screen television hanging on the wall. The popular daily game show was interrupted with a news flash. "This is breaking news: early this morning, dignitary Ambassador John Dorn was involved in a serious automobile accident. There were reports of one fatality.

The Ambassador's chauffeur Samuel Moore was killed in the crash, while others involved were taken to John Hopkins Hospital."

"My God …" said Maggie. "Mary had to be with them. I thought Samuel Moore had left DC? John Dorn is a fucking liar."

"Walking over to his suitcase and pulling out some jeans, Daniels said,

"Yeah … well … Moore has left DC now! That's for damn sure!"

"Okay!" said Maggie. "I guess we have no choice but to tell Professor Hans about the accident and everything else that has been going on since we got here. Unless he already knows about the accident and that's what this meeting is all about?" said Bill Moss.

"Guys would you please hurry up and get dressed?" demanded Maggie.

Knowing the seriousness of the moment Bill got up off the floor and went down the hall to his bedroom, while Glenn pulled some pants and a sweatshirt out of his duffel bag on the floor. Maggie sat hypnotized by the television news story being repeated over and over as the hour passed. Larry and Glenn, fully dressed, turned their attention back to the news story. Coming down the hallway fastening his belt, Moss said, "Hey guys, I'm ready!"

The three men grabbed their jackets and followed Maggie out the door. The four hurried down the hallway to Professor Hans' room. As they reach the door they saw it was cracked open. Pushing the door all the way open. Maggie said. "Professor Hans?" Taking his turn, Glenn Taste yelled

"Dr. Hans?"

"Nobody's here," said Larry Daniels, coming through the door and looking around. Picking up some of the Professor's papers off his desk, he looked at them for a moment, rearranged them and putting them back.

"Maybe he just stepped out. Somebody call his cell phone."

The Other Life of Mary Abrams | 149

Paranoia setting in, Maggie said, "Moss, go check the bedroom! And I'll call the Professor."

Moss' facial expression was followed by, "I'm not going back there!"

"Larry?" said Maggie.

"Larry what?" said Daniels, knowing she wanted him to go check the Professor's bedroom.

"Hey bro, fuck it … I'll go!" said Glenn Taste as he walked over to the kitchen sink getting a butter knife out of the drawer. He headed down the hall.

Maggie took out her cell phone and began calling the Professor's number.

"Dammit, there's no answer," said Maggie, leaving a voice message.

"Prof Hans would you please call me as soon as possible? It's an emergency."

Within minutes Glenn was back. "Nothing. Although his bed was slept in! No notes or anything."

"Maybe he's at the hospital?" said Maggie.

"This is some strange shit!" said Larry, getting angry. " Mary's in the hospital and Dr. Hans has disappeared! What the fuck!"

The mentioning of Mary's name rekindled Maggie's emotions, to the point where she began crying.

"Slowly walking over and putting his arm around her," Bill Moss said softly. "Everything's gonna be okay."

"Thanks Bill," Maggie said, hugging him and wiping her eyes. I better go get some clothes for Mary. She's going to need a change of clothes."

Brushing her hair back she regained her composure and told the guys she would be back in a few minutes.

"If Professor Hans is not back by the time Maggie comes back, We're leaving!" said Larry Daniels, picking up some papers off the floor.

"I concur with that my bro," said Glenn Taste, as he walked over to the window.

150 | James Edwards III

Quietly, Bill Moss walked over to the refrigerator and opened it. Finding an apple, he began eating it. It wasn't long before Maggie returned, knocking on the door and then pushing it open.

"You guys ready? I got her stuff," Maggie said, holding up a large black plastic bag.

"Ready as we'll ever be!" said Larry as he turned and followed Maggie out the door. Closely trailing them were Bill and Glenn. Glenn, being last, reached back and closed the door. Rushing down the hallway to the elevator, they took it down to the first floor out to the lobby into the parking lot. Locating the van, they all climbed in and buckled up. Anxious to get to the hospital, Larry caused the tires to squeal as they pulled away. The college van rushed through the traffic, maneuvering to get to its destination as fast as possible. Slowing down for a traffic jam, Bill Moss hollered, "Pull over here for a minute!"

"For what?" said Larry frowning.

"I need to stop at that store!" Bill said, unbuckling his seat belt.

"What fucking store?" demanded Larry.

"Stewart electronics. I need something for my computer."

"Dammit Bill," said Maggie. "We don't have time for this shit. We need to get to the hospital!"

"Hey, what the hell guys? We're stuck in traffic anyway!" said Glenn Taste, defending Moss. "Let him run in there and grabbed what he needs."

Shaking his head and taking a deep breath, Larry said. " Fuck it. Go ahead."

Unlocking the door, Moss grabbed the side door handle, and slid it back. Jumping out of the van, he ran into the store. Traffic slowly began to move but no more than a car's length. Five minutes passing brought Bill Moss out of the store. Noticing the van had moved down. He hurriedly walked to it. Glenn opened the door and he climbed in and re-buckled his seat belt just as traffic began to clear. As traffic began to flow it wasn't long before the students had crossed over from Virginia into Baltimore, arriving The Other Life of Mary Abrams | 151

at John Hopkins. Finding the visitors' parking lot, they parked the van.

Unbuckling and getting out, Maggie grabbed the bag of extra clothes for Mary. The students rushed into the hospital to the information counter.

With the guys looking on Maggie asked, "Can you tell me if Mary Abrams is still in emergency? She was in a car accident with the dignitary Ambassador John Dorn."

"Yes ... I'm much aware of the accident. Mary Abrams," said the woman at the informational counter. "Mnmn ... let me look that up. No ... she's been transferred to the ICU upstairs in room 411, said the elderly lady with glasses. "Go down this hallway and take the elevator on your left."

"Thank you!" said Maggie. "Was Ambassador Dorn hospitalized?"

"No, he wasn't," said the receptionist. "He left the hospital several hours ago."

Maggie thanked her again and led the guys down the red striped hallway like Joan of Arc leading her troops. Finding the elevator on the left they took it up to the fourth floor. They looked for room number 411.

Finding it, they were startled to see Mary lying there unconscious. Maggie began crying as the guys circled the bed.

The emotional moment was interrupted by an intensive care nurse.

"Is everything okay?" asked the nurse seeing everyone upset.

"How long has she been like this?" asked Larry Daniels, taking off his jacket.

"Since she was admitted!" said the nurse. "Are you her family?"

Half stuttering Maggie said, "No, just friends and classmates." She handed Mary's extra clothes to Bill Moss to put in the drawer. "Can you tell us what's wrong with her?"

"Nothing physical. It seems she's in some kind of shock. The only explanation is the accident."

"There's nothing they can do?" Bill Moss said, wringing his hands.

"No, I'm sorry," said the nurse, picking up some soiled linen. "Just keep talking to her. She can hear you. If there's anything you need just 152 | James Edwards III

press the button on the side of her bed." Picking up the linen she had collected, she exited the room.

"Aww bro, this isn't good," said Glenn Taste, turning toward the window.

"No, it's not," said Larry, taking Mary's hand. "Mary … Mary …

wake up!"

"That's not going to help, Larry!" said Maggie, getting upset. "We just have to wait until she comes out of it. I'm not leaving her side. Why don't you guys go back to the hotel and wait for Dr. Hans? And I'll stay here in case she wakes up." As she was speaking, Mary began moaning, getting the attention of her classmates. Opening her eyes and staring at Maggie she uttered, "Chosen …"

The surprise and excitement that Mary had come to was short-lived, as she drifted back into a state of unconsciousness. "See guys! Things aren't as bad as they look."

Encouraged by Mary's awakening the guys decided to take Maggie's advice and returned to the hotel, leaving Maggie to watch over Mary. They left the hospital.

The Other Life of Mary Abrams | 153

Chapter 18:

Going Home

Arriving back at the Hey-Adams Hotel the young college men valeted the van. Climbing out, Larry took a ticket from the parking attendant while Glenn and Bill waited at the lobby door.

"Hey guys," said Larry walking toward them. "You guys wanta go see if Dr. Hans is back? While I jump in the shower."

"No problem., bro!" said Glenn Taste, giving him a fist pump.

Walking behind the two, Bill Moss mumbled, "Why do we have to go?"

The three caught the elevator up to the third floor where they departed.

Daniels went to their hotel room while Bill and Glenn headed down the hallway. Reaching the Professor's hotel room, they found the door closed but not locked. They called out as they opened it: "Professor Hans! Professor …"

"He's not back," said Bill Moss, peeking down the hallway leading to the bedroom.

"Where the hell could he be?" said Glenn, walking over to the desk where Larry was rumbling through the Professor's papers. Picking them up, he paused for several minutes and said, "Hey … look at this! Here's some astrological charts."

"What," said Bill, growing inquisitive. Staring at one of the pages, he saw a list of all the Ambassadors that were at the summit. "What …

The Other Life of Mary Abrams | 155

the … hell?" Suddenly the door swung open and Larry Daniels marched in.

"Is he here?" asked Larry, shoving past Bill.

"Damn that was quick," Bill said, noticing Larry's dry hair.

Ignoring Moss, Larry asked, "What you got there, Glenn?"

"Just some papers, that's all bro," said Glenn, as he examined them.

Larry walked over and took the papers out of Glenn's hands.

"Hey!" said Glenn, surprised by Larry abruptness.

"Don't fuck with any of his personal shit," said Larry, becoming agitated. "He's not here. Let's go!"

As they were leaving, Glenn took one of the Professor's papers without Larry knowing it. The three men left and closed the door behind them, going back to their hotel room. Swiping his key card, Larry opened the door.

Bill walked over to his book bag and took out his computer and sat in the floor. Glenn followed Larry to the kitchen area. Reaching into the refrigerator Larry asked. "You wanta beer?"

"Yeah bro … Cool!" said Glenn, taking the beer and popping it open.

"You know, maybe, we should call the police?"

"I don't think it's that serious! Look, we found Mary! Professor Hans will show up soon," said Larry with confidence.

Taking a swig of beer Glenn said, "When? He shoulda' been back by now!"

"He'll be back, you'll see," said Larry, gulping beer down and walking over to the sofa, sitting down and putting his feet up on the coffee table.

Bill Moss closed his computer. Taking a pillow from the sofa, he put it under his head and fell asleep on the floor. Before long Larry and Glenn had dozed off. The three slept sound as the afternoon rolled into the evening. Larry Daniels, being the first to wake up, leaned over and shook Glenn sitting next to him. "Hey Glenn. Wake up man!"

156 | James Edwards III

"Yeah, yeah bro, I'm woke," said Glenn sitting up and yawning.

Larry, taking a pillow out from behind him, threw it and hit Moss lying on the floor. "Hey Mossy! Wake the fuck up!"

Moss sat up and looked around, rubbing his eyes. "What's up guys?"

Moss said, getting up off the floor.

"Shit!" said Larry. "We've overslept. We gotta go back to the hospital and see how Mary is doing."

Glenn and Bill took turns showering while Larry sat on the sofa watching TV.

Glenn finished dressing and the two waited on Bill Moss coming out of the bathroom walking into the living room with his shirt unbuttoned and belt hanging out of the belt loops.Bill said, "I'm ready!"

"If you say so," said Glenn Taste, standing up and walking over to the sink, getting a glass of water. He drank the water down and said, "Let's go." The three headed out the door down the hall to the elevator to the first floor out the door to the valet. The parking attendant brought the Rental van around. Larry tipped the guy and climbed in the drivers' seat, while Bill and Glenn got in and buckled up.

A half hour later, they arrived at John Hopkins, parking the van in the visitors parking lot.

Walking to the entrance Bill asked, "Whata we gonna do? We're supposed be going home tomorrow night."

"Well," said Glenn Taste, "I don't know what you're gonna do, but I plan to be on that plane tomorrow night."

"Really Glenn? Really!" said Larry. "We can't leave Mary here! What's wrong with you?"

And expression of guilt crossed Glenn's face. He gave no verbal response while fixing his ponytail. Entering the Hospital, the three took the hallway with the red directional stripe down to the elevator doors on the left. The doors opened and the students got on and pressed the fourth floor. Getting off, they found their way down the hall to room 411. Walk-The Other Life of Mary Abrams | 157

ing into the room, Larry saw Maggie sleeping in a recliner chair. He walked over and shook her. "Hey Mag wake up!"

Stirring out of her sleep and opening her eyes, she said "Hey guys."

"Where's Mary? Did she wake up?" said Larry enthusiastically, as he sat down in the other recliner.

Sitting up, Maggie looked around and saw Mary's empty hospital bed.

Jumping up, Maggie ran into the bathroom, looking for Mary. With perplexed looks, Glenn and Bill stood there like statues.

"She's not in the bathroom. She must've woken up. I, I guess I dozed off!" said Maggie, taking the blame for not knowing where Mary was. "But I never left that chair!"

"No need to panic, Mag" said Larry. "The nurse probably took her down for some tests."

"I hope you're right," said Maggie, straightening herself up from sleeping in the chair.

"I'll go check the nurses' station," said Bill Moss trying to help.

"Yeah. That 'll work Bro! Make yourself useful," Glenn said as he looked around Mary's room.

Bill Moss left the room and hurried down the hallway to the nurse's station.

Four floors down in the basement of the hospital, the brother of Ambassador John Dorn, Ambassador James Dorn was in the morgue with

Samuel Moore, lying on a gurney. Ambassador James Dorn raised his hands over the body of Moore, falling into a trance, Dorn began to pray in Hebrew. Laying hands on Samuel Moore, he began to glow blinding bright like the sun. Suddenly his chest began to move up and down. Moore opened his eyes. Barely able to speak, he said, "Praise God" in Hebrew and asked, "How long was I gone?"

"Not long," said Ambassador James Dorn.

Dorn helped Moore off the table. Cracking the door open to see if the coast was clear, they quickly left the morgue.

158 | James Edwards III

Back at the nurses' station, Bill said, "Excuse me ma'am but my classmate Mary Abrams is in Room 411. Can you tell me if the orderly came and got her for tests?"

"Just a minute, sir!" said the young blonde nurse as she checked the register. "No ...no, she didn't go down for tests. She was discharged from the hospital a few hours ago."

"What!" said Bill, feeling his blood pressure rising. Hearing the elevator doors opened behind him. He turned around to see the doors closing with Samuel Moore and Ambassador James Dorn standing in the elevator.

His face turning as white as a ghost. He became speechless.

"Excuse me sir? Is there anything else I can do for you?" said the young nurse as he turned back around to face her. Not being able to say anything, he rushed down the hallway to Room 411.

Bill rushed into the room. Stuttering and shaking, he blurted out, "Hey guys ..." Mary has been discharged. And that ain't all! Samuel Moore is still alive!"

"What?" said Maggie.

Glenn Taste, looking shocked said, "Hey dude, are you for real?"

"Yes," said Bill wringing his hands as he began sweating and shaking with fear. "I saw him and one of the other Ambassadors on the elevator."

"Get the fuck out of here!" said Larry, standing up and becoming heated.

"He can't be alive," said Maggie. "The news reported him dead!"

"Well he's not," said Bill, picking up a towel and wiping the sweat off his face.

"Why would they say he was killed in the car crash if he wasn't!" said Maggie.

"None of this makes any sense," exclaimed Glenn Taste. "Are you sure that was him bro?" Before Bill could respond, Larry added to the conversation, "Maybe you thought it was him?"

"I know what I saw," said Bill, calming down.

The Other Life of Mary Abrams | 159

"If Moore is alive, then he knows where Mary is. We've got to find him."

"And how do you propose to do that? " said Larry staring at Maggie.

"I don't know?" said Maggie sadly as she dropped her face into her hands.

"There's no need to search for a dead guy to help us find Mary!" Said Bill Moss regaining control of his emotions. "We can find her."

"How? Where do we look?" said Glenn Taste. "This is a big ass city!"

Moving the food caddy out of the way, Moss said with hints of mystery in his voice. "We can find her!" Check her drawer and see if she put on the clothes we brought,

Maggie jumped up and start rummaging through the hospital drawers.

"There gone! All the clothes I brought are gone!"

"Now what?" said Larry. "We knew she had to wear something out the hospital."

Smiling, Bill said, "That's why I put a tracking device in the cuff of her jeans."

"What?" said Maggie, stopping her search and turning to Bill Moss.

"That's why you stopped at the electronics store?" Maggie rushed over to Bill, hugging him around the neck and kissing him on the cheek. "Bill I love you!" she said.

"Okay," said Larry. "Now you're telling us that you put a bug in Mary's clothes?"

"Exactly," Moss said, feeling superior, while rubbing his stomach.

"Cool, bro! You the man!" Glenn said, jumping up, high-fiving Bill Moss.

"Okay … So how does it work?" said Maggie, getting anxious.

"I can track her with my laptop," said Bill, holding up his computer.

"Great!" said Maggie. "Finally, someone is thinking!"

"Let's not waste any more time," Larry said with authority. "Hey Mossy, turn that thing on! "

160 | James Edwards III

Ignoring the nickname. Moss decided to hold back on his famous index finger pose. He responded, "I will when we get to the van!" Deep down inside, Bill reveled in the fact that his classmates had to depend him. For once he was leading the group. The college students rearranged the room the way they found it and left. Rushing down the hallway with the red directional stripe, they came to the elevator where Moss said he saw Samuel Moore and Ambassador James Dorn.

"This elevator right here!" said Moss, pointing at the door. The doors suddenly opened and Moss jumped back only to see an empty elevator.

"Come on bro," said Glenn chuckling. "Ain't nobody in there!" Not knowing what to say, Maggie and Larry didn't react. Maggie, Larry and Glenn entered the elevator and waited on Moss. Somewhat hesitant, he slowly walked in. Taking the elevator down to the first floor, the students exited and rushed out to the parking lot to find the van. Climbing in and closing the door, they all sat patiently as Bill Moss opened and programmed his computer.

"Okay," said Bill excited. "I'm locked in."

"So how do we pick up the signal?" asked Maggie, looking at Bill in the rearview mirror.

"I think we need to take a vote. Do we start the search here in Baltimore or should we drive back to DC?"

Bill's classmates said in harmony, "Back to Washington."

"Okay," said Glenn. "We all agree; let's go." Larry started the van and they pulled out of the parking lot. Merging into the flowing traffic, they headed back to Washington DC.

"Hey," said Glenn Taste. "Wouldn't Ambassador Dorn have an office in the capital building?"

"I would think so," said Maggie, looking out the window as they were getting closer to the Congressional building.

"No we're not," said Maggie reading Glenn's mind. "We're not breaking into any federal building, let alone Congress."

The Other Life of Mary Abrams | 161

"Yeah," said Larry, not finishing his sentence as he was interrupted by a beeping noise.

"I think I got something," said Bill, leaning closer to the computer screen.

"Where is it coming from?" said Maggie looking over her shoulder.

"I'm not sure, but we're headed in the right direction. The signal is getting stronger."

As they crossed over the Potomac into Washington DC, Bill Moss said,

"Make a right here and go down to 11th Street and make a left." As they followed Bill's direction, they drew closer to the White House.

"Holy … shit the signal seems to be coming from the White House!"

"Couldn't be," said Larry, brushing his blond hair out of the face.

"Are you sure Bill?" asked Maggie.

"I'm pretty sure," said Bill, double checking.

"All bro, this is fucked up," said Glenn, fidgeting in his seat.

"This is crazy," said Larry Daniels. "It doesn't make any sense. Why would she be at the White House?"

"I'm with you Larry. All of this is just insane," said Maggie.

Leaning forward from the back seat, Glenn asked Maggie, 'So what's next?"

"I don't know," said Maggie, trying to think. "Larry, find a parking spot and pull over."

Driving another half block from the White House, Larry found a place to park. Pulling over, he turned the motor off and looked at Maggie. "So

…now what?"

"So we wait," said Maggie, unbuckling her seat belt and getting comfortable. Realizing she was serious, her remaining classmates followed suit.

Before long they had all dozed off.

162 | James Edwards III

Chapter 19:

Mary Abrams

The night went deeper into darkness as large black thunderous clouds rolled in over the city. This night was different; the warm and cold air in competition with one another fought it out, causing lightning flashes and sonic booms that woke the college students' sleep in the van. BOOM …

CRACKLE … BOOM, BOOM.

"Holy shit! What was that?" Maggie said, realizing it was a lightning storm. "Dammit, we felt asleep!"

Rubbing his eyes, Bill hadn't realized that while he was asleep, he closed the computer.

As Larry woke up he started the van and let the window down for fresh air.

Glenn Taste yawned and asked, "What time is it?"

Fully awake Maggie looked at her watch. "Close to 11," she said. Turning around, she asked Bill Moss, "Do we still have a signal?" Not wanting them to know he had accidentally closed the laptop while sleeping, he quickly opened it and punched in some numbers. Suddenly, the beeping started again. Hearing the signal, Maggie turned back around and asked,

"Anybody hungry?"

"I'm okay," said Larry, letting the window back up.

The Other Life of Mary Abrams | 163

Glenn, knowing Bill didn't want to mention food, spoke up."Yeah we could use something to eat," said Glenn, smiling at Bill knowing he was hungry.

"Well we passed a small deli on the corner in the next block," said Larry.

"Well!" said Maggie. "Let's go! Everybody buckle up!"

Larry, pulling out, put on the turn signal to get in traffic.

"Wait a minute guys," said Bill Moss, getting excited. "The signal is getting stronger." Puzzled, Bill said, "It's coming toward us."

"What?" said Larry. As he was speaking, a parade of black SUVs with red and blue emergency lights flashing began passing them. As the last SUV passed. The signal on Bill's computer went high pitch as the President's limousine went by, identified by the US flags on the car.

"There they go," said Maggie. "Larry, turn around!"

Larry drove half a block and made a U-turn, following the parade of dignitaries.

"Where do you think, they're headed?" said Glenn Taste.

"Who knows," said Daniels. "Something's up for them to be leaving the White House at this hour."

"Bill," said Maggie. "Are you sure the signal is coming from one of the cars?"

"I'm sure," said Bill. "Just keep driving!"

Larry followed the caravan through the darkened streets of Washington only to end up at the Capitol Building. Staying their distance, they watched the SUVs pull into the parking lot. Parking close to one another, they lined up like checkers on a checker board.

"Go around the block Larry!" said Maggie. "They must be having a late emergency Congress meeting."

"You think we might be able to slip in unnoticed?" asked Glenn.

"That's exactly what were gonna do!" said Maggie. "We're going in as congressional pages."

164 | James Edwards III

"That's ridiculous," said Larry. "How do you propose to do that?"

Maggie answered. "There's an all-night Xerox store on Pennsylvania Avenue," said Maggie. "We're going to make our own badges and attend that meeting."

"That'll work," said Bill Moss nervously, not wanting the adventure.

Larry headed back to the Xerox store on Pennsylvania Avenue, pulling up in front and parking. Maggie got out and ran in. She was back within 20 minutes.

"A piece of cake guys," she said, climbing in the van with four matching shirts and passing them out along with counterfeit page badges.

"How did you get the shirts?" said Larry sitting up.

"You don't want to know!" Maggie Werks said, with a devilish smile.

"All right fellas let's do it," Maggie, feeling good, leaned over and kissed Larry on the cheek. Daniels drove the short distance back to the congressional building. Pulling in the parking lot away from all the black SUVs.

They sat quietly with the motor running.

"Look guys act normal. Don't bring on any suspicion. Put your shirts and badges on and leave your jackets in the van."

"What about the computer?" asked Moss, not wanting to leave it.

"Of course. Bring it!" said Maggie, short-tempered.

The college men began obeying as if they were listening to their mother, taking off their jackets and sticking their badges on the shirts Maggie gave them.

They checked for last-minute details and climbed out of the van, locking the door and taking the familiar steps leading up to the Capitol Building. Up the steps where the ushers greeted them the first day of the summit, they entered the building into the reception center.

"Okay Mag.," said Larry Daniels, "It's your call."

Glenn and Bill, with mouths hanging open, stood waiting for direction.

"Look, we gotta find Mary! She must be in here! Right Bill?" Maggie said, looking for support.

The Other Life of Mary Abrams | 165

Put on the spot, Bill Moss boldly said, "This is where the signal led us and it's still sending out frequency. This is the location believe me."

"Okay, all phones on vibrate," said Maggie. "If anyone sees anything suspicious don't call but text. Got it?" Everyone agreeing, Maggie said,

"All right boys. Let's mingle." Pretending to be pages, they started brief conversations with some of the dignitaries, assisting them any way they could, hoping to finding Mary.

As the time began to wear into the night, and determined to find her classmate, Maggie searched the different hallways until she found Ambassadors Dorn's office.

Seeing his name on the door, she was overjoyed and could hardly contain herself as she sent a multi-text message to her classmates. "Eureka!

Level below the rotunda, come at once."

Arriving first was Glenn Taste. "Mag You down here?" whispered Glenn as he approached the Office Door of Ambassador John Dorn.

"Come on in...." Maggie said. "And be quiet; a security guard just walked through here right before you came."

"Okay," said Glenn closing the door slowly so he wouldn't make any noise.

"What did you find?" Glenn said, barely audible as he moved toward Maggie in the dark office only lit by moonlight shining through the blinds.

Shining a small flashlight she had taken out of her purse, Maggie said,

"Over here, look like some kind of ancient scrolls and letters to the guest speakers of the summit."

One of the letters that Maggie was holding looked familiar to Glenn.

It was an exact duplicate of the one taken off the Professor's desk in his hotel room, stamped with some ancient symbol.

"Stop shaking Mag, and please hold the light still!" Glenn said examined the paper further.

Suddenly they heard a noise at the door, turning the flash light off, they hid behind the desk. Looking over it, they could see Bill Moss's head peeking in the door.

166 | James Edwards III

"Dammit, Bill," said Maggie, "you're gonna give us a heart attack."

"Yeah bro!" said Glenn standing up from behind the desk.

"Sorry," said Bill, as he moved toward them in the moonlit room, knocking over a small trash can as he got closer.

"Careful," said Maggie, getting angry.

"Where the hell is Larry?" said Maggie.

"I don't know?" said Bill, his voice quivering. "You know he doesn't like taking orders."

Ignoring the two, Glenn focused in on the letter. "Hey guys, look at this? " Holding the letter up he showed them: Ambassador Dorn

Ambassador Ivanoff

Ambassador Sandoval

Ambassador Creses

Ambassador Isser

Ambassador Peres

Ambassador Levitt

Ambassador Elbaz

Ambassador Salinger

Looking intensely, Maggie and Bill said in harmony, "It's a list of their names."

"More than that," said Glenn Taste. "Read the first letter of their last names."

Maggie, deciphering it before Moss, said, "It spells *Disciples* but it's only nine letters and it's 11 Ambassadors."

"Yeah, that's what I thought too, until I realized you got two set of brothers; that makes eleven.

"Disciples of what?" said Bill. "In the Bible, there were twelve. Who are these guys?"

The Other Life of Mary Abrams | 167

"That's in the Bible, bro. This is real life!" said Glenn, looking Moss in the face.

The sounds of a car ignition's starting up from outside took their attention away from their discovery. The three walked over to the window and peeked out the blinds.

"Hell," said Maggie, they're all leaving. At that moment, the office door seemed to open in slow motion. There stood a silhouette in the doorway.

"Larry?" said Maggie. "It's about time you got your ass here." The figure walked over to the light switch and turned it on.

Standing in shock with white faces, the college students couldn't speak.

They stood there staring at Samuel Moore. Walking halfway toward them he motioned for them to leave the room. They shook as they walked past him out the door. He closed the door behind him and locked it. The students were afraid to look in his face as they moved to the side of the hallway when he walked through. Motioning them to follow him, Moore took them down the hallway through a secret passage that led up to the house chambers. Upon entering the chambers, the students saw it was totally empty. They wondered where all the people had gone so quickly. In the shadows stood the President of the United States with Secret Service. Sitting in the speakers' chair was Ambassador John Dorn.

Standing up, he walked down to the main floor where the students were, dismissing Samuel Moore. He said, "Welcome. We've been expecting you!" with a mysterious smile as he approached them. "College forti-tude," Dorn said, "I love it! We knew you wouldn't give up! At that moment, Mary came out of the left wing walking slowly toward them.

Trailing her were the Ten Summit Ambassadors. Seeing her, Maggie cried out, "Mary!" Mary knew Maggie had been worried. Mary walked over to her with a strange expression and said. "My child."

"What," said Maggie. "Have you lost your mind? We thought you were kidnapped! What the hell is going on here and how did you become friends with a dead man."

168 | James Edwards III

"That's right Mary!" said Glenn Taste. "Moore has risen from the dead!"

Moss stood there speechless, staring at the two. But thought. "something's wrong."

"Shall I … Mother?" said Ambassador Dorn. Mary nodded and waved her hand.

"'There are mysteries in life that we are unaware of and sometimes strange things happen. As guardians of the world, we must be prepared for the unseen. And without controversy, great is the mystery of godliness.'

My brother Timothy wrote that over 2000 years ago," said Dorn, turning to look at Ambassador Thaddeus (Timothy) Ivanoff and smiling. "We are the original disciples of Christ. The Father has reincarnated us to open the dimensional portal for His return."

"You people are crazy," said Maggie. "What the hell do your rituals have the do with us?"

"I believe Mary can explain that to you," said Ambassador John Dorn, the disciple that wrote Revelations.

"I know it's hard to grasp all of this," said Mary with sympathy. "But I knew all along and never discussed it with anyone. My knowledge of the past. The Father has chosen me again. I am blessed over all women, to be chosen a second time to bring the Messiah back to earth. All of you have passed lives that tie to the gospel of Christ. In time, you will remember for the Father has called all of you into service." As Mary was speaking, Dr.

Luas Hans came out from behind a column.

The students were shocked to see him and wondered if he could explain all this.

"And you, Professor?" said Maggie becoming afraid, as the Professor drew closer.

"I'm sorry that all of this has caused you emotional duress," said Professor Hans.

"We all have lived before! The dreams showed me," said the Professor.

"For I am the apostle Paul, chosen by the Father to bring you here. Mary The Other Life of Mary Abrams | 169

is needed to complete the circle. It's our mission! I know it seems confusing, but we're all just recycled souls coming to earth over, and over again, until the Father's kingdom is established."

As he spoke, a methodical walking Larry Daniels came out of the shadows from under the balcony, slowly walking down, the main aisle.

"Well… . said Ambassador Peter Creses. "We knew you would show up!"

Turning around to look, Larry's classmates hollered out. "Larry, what the hell is going on?"

"Don't call me that!" said Larry, his face displaying anger.

"No," said Ambassador Thomas Salinger, "Don't call him that. He's used to being call by his real name. Let me introduce you to … Judas of Iscarot"

Maggie gasped while Bill and Glenn looked at each other in dismay.

Becoming indignant Larry said, "I have every right to be here just like all of you!"

"No! You don't, said Ambassador Peter Creses. "You're a fucking trai-tor and have no part in this return."

"And who appointed you leader, Peter? And you, Thomas, how dare you? You doubted that the Messiah had risen." The apostle Ambassador (John) Dorn interrupted with authority.

"Judas! Judas of Iscarot, you are dismissed! You have no part!" Ambassador Peter Creses commanded the other disciples into a half circle.

They dropped 30 pieces of silver as a barrier between Larry (Judas), Daniels and themselves.

John signaled the other disciples. They raised their hands toward Larry, Judas, Daniels and began speaking Hebrew. Screaming and cursing, Daniels (Judas) couldn't cross the barrier.

Tears flowing down his face, he turned around screaming and ran out of the building. Appearing again was Samuel Moore. He walked over to Mary and bowed down, taking her by the arm, he escorted her over to the 170 | James Edwards III

half circle. Turning to the remaining students he told them to step back.

The Secret Service stood in front of the President of the United States who had been an intricate part of the entire thing.

As Samuel Moore began backing up, Maggie Werks asked him, "Who are you?"

With sincerity, he said, "I was a spectator that was in the crowd when the Messiah was passing by and could no longer carry his cross. The Roman soldiers chose me to carry it to Golgotha where he was crucified.

But they didn't choose me … God did!"

As he finished speaking the eleven disciples formed the circle with Mary stepping in to complete it. The house of chambers took on a spiritual dimension as a ball of white light, appearing from nowhere, began glowing brighter and brighter. In the center of the circle, as the light permeated the room, Mary (the mother of Jesus) Abrams went into a trance, her eyes rolled back in her head as she began speaking in Hebrew, suddenly she could feel an embryo forming inside her. The light moved throughout the entire room, rising to the ceiling. From the outside, the light could be seen shining through The Dome of the Capital up to the Heavens.

Revelation 22:12-13: "And behold, I come quickly and any reward is wit me to give every man according as his work shall be. I am Alpha and

Omega, the beginning and the end, the first and the last."

The Other Life of Mary Abrams | 171

Edwards D CXNS TO FINAL 3 - 071718.qxp_Layout 1 7/17/18 9:43 AM
Page 172

Table of Contents